I0761052

FIREBRAND'S CUPID

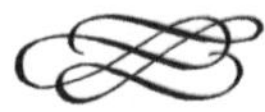

NIKI MITCHELL

This is a work of fiction. Names, characters, places, and incidents are the product of the author's imagination or are used fictitiously. Any resemblance to actual persons living or dead, business establishments, events, or location is entirely coincidental. This publisher does not have any control and does not assume responsibility for the author or third-party website or their content.

Printed in the United States of America

❀ Created with Vellum

Firebrand's Cupid is dedicated to my friends and family who always support my crazy ideas.

FIREBRAND'S CUPID

A Contemporary Love Story with a Light Paranormal Twist

When a Cupid archer loses his magical ability while on Earth, he ends up falling for an athletic, alluring mortal.

Zander Eros has the perfect life—until his Cupid fiancé dumps him. He gets tossed in an Idaho jail, ending up with no magical powers and no way to get home. But when he meets a gorgeous, off-limits human, it turns out that she's a match made in heaven.

Ivy Venturi loves skateboarding down the streets in a beautiful resort town in Idaho.

She doesn't need to get sidetracked from her studies.

She doesn't need a handsome hunk to take her hiking and paddle boarding and ziplining.

But Zander steals her heart—and then he leaves town.

CHAPTER 1

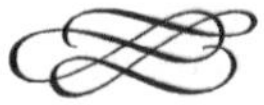

The Realm of Cupid's Corner

On the outskirts of town, Zander Eros floated down to a grassy meadow near Aphrodite's Lake. He unfurled his wings, plucked a crooked feather, swirled his magical ruby dust from his fingertips, and turned his glittery sky-blue wings black. Black matched his cheerless mood. He peered over the edge of a cumulus cloud to Earth, guzzling from a bottle of Hennessy brandy brought from the world below. Taking a long swig, bitterness filled his thoughts—all because of his two-timing ex, Cami Calypso.

The little Cupid crushed their carefully laid plans, plans that originated when they were cherub neighbors. Their marriage was expected. The idea perpetuated by both the Eros and Calypso families. He and Cami were both attractive and exceptional marksman. They'd been deemed the Golden

Archers. Their children would be extraordinary, their life perfect.

Curse Cami for saying she never loved him. Curse her for choosing a *human* over him and marrying a cowboy just yesterday. Curse her father for giving his blessing. A sharp pain dug deep in his heart. Her father used to treat Zander like a son, but that would stop now that he wouldn't be a part of Cami's life. Fury blazed inside his mind as he polished off the last drop of brandy and propelled the bottled toward the lake. It hit a boulder near the shoreline and shattered into broken pieces—shattered much like his future.

Why had she worn his ring if she didn't want to marry him? Everyone in town knew about the engagement. Once word got out about her choosing a mortal, he'd be looked down on by society. His social standing would be in question. The concept made his stomach turn.

Cami *should* love *him*, not a *human.*

A message flashed on his wrist heart emblem.

Holy shit.

He had an Earthly assignment to complete. Two hours before sunset—on a Sunday, no less. His last assignment, and he'd have over a month off.

His head was a bit fuzzy. What did it matter? He'd been a champion archer since the age of ten and never missed a target on purpose. At least the task should be fast and easy. According to the couple's profile, they needed a love boost. Shooting arrows filled with a love potion when his own love life was in shambles. Hypocrisy at its finest. If only Cupids could receive love boosts. Cami would realize her mistake.

Once he fixed the doomed couple's relationship, then what? Since his best friend recently moved to Lover's Landing, he had nowhere to go. Nobody to hang with. Nothing to do except spend time with his new pal, Hennessy. While on Earth, he could easily find a bar or saloon in town and pretend to be a human for the night. He might as well drink where nobody knew him. Failing to snag the expected wife, he wasn't ready to face his community.

He flew above the dirt path through the Calypso Forest.

Calypso.

The forest named after one of Cami's ancestors.

He couldn't wait to get far away from this realm to regroup and figure out a new game plan. As he took the fork to the left away from the giant redwoods, a violet cuckoo perched on a branch. Its distinct call annoyed him like the cuckoo clock on the wall in his den.

Rays of light flickered on the Fates River. This sunbeam would take him to Moosehead, Idaho. He glided to the edge, opened his wings wide, and wrapped his arms around the radiant column. The speed sobered him.

Cursed chaos, he approached the hotel too fast.

Pushing his wings in close to his body, they failed to slow his descent through the roof of the Moosehead Lodge. He skidded to a stop on top of an oak mantle secured to a massive stone fireplace. The tips of his shoes tapped against a silver-framed photo. It wobbled precariously close to the edge and stopped.

Luckily, the two people behind the concierge counter were engrossed in their conversation and didn't look in his direction. Whew!

Wiping a bead of sweat from his brow, he breathed in deeply. Baked goods overrode the scent of pine. He glanced at the people seated on couches and chairs, across the shiny wooden floor to the customers on bar stools drinking. No amber-colored auras. No signs of a distressed couple. His assignment should be around here somewhere.

The front door swung open.

"If you loved me ..." a man's voice yelled from outside.

Bingo. He'd found the couple.

Now to recall the couple's file. He tapped his heart emblem on his wrist, pulled up a virtual screen, and skimmed the info.

Married for five years, the wife gave all her attention to their two kids. He felt neglected. This was their first time leaving the kids for a weekend.

The front door opened, allowing him to flutter outside under the veranda.

"You don't want a wife, you want a cook and housekeeper," a woman snarled.

Their love lights faded. A love boost would allow her to see that her husband longed for affection.

Time to complete his task. He took his quiver and bow

off his shoulder, snatched a silver arrow, nocked it in place, and floated lower.

The wife stood facing her husband with her hands on her hips. "I'm going to call the sitter."

Zander moved a few feet from her, saw the perfect angle, and released his arrow. Zing. Dark pink lit her heart.

"I love you. I miss holding you at night," the man said.

Her expression softened. "I miss you, too."

He pulled her into his arms, and they were kissing.

Success.

Normally, Zander would be overjoyed. Another tally to add to his chart, but today his completed task seemed flat. He flew to the side of the Moosehead Lodge to transform into his human size, floated to the ground, swirled magical dust from his fingertips, and his body grew larger. He flicked more dust and jeans and a golf shirt formed around him, followed by black Ralph Lauren loafers.

Across the street, lights from the Bison Tavern flashed and caught Zander's attention. A drink sounded perfect.

With dusk settling on the horizon, people continued taking selfies in front of a bison statue. Others ambled along the sidewalk in T-shirts or light sweatshirts. Not a bad place for vacationers out on a stroll.

A handful of vehicles parked in the slots lining the main street. Half a dozen cars passed by. A monster-sized truck pulled into a parking lot behind the back of the building.

Like it mattered how many mortals were around—he had nowhere important to go. Strolling across the street, he couldn't believe someone hung real antlers on the façade surrounding the Bison Tavern sign. He strode up planked steps, opened a squeaky door, walked into a long rectangular room, went up to the bar and squeezed in-between a couple of men in cowboy hats.

CHAPTER 2

"What'll it be?" the bartender asked.

"Hennessy."

The bartender poured the amber liquid into a snifter. "That'll be five dollars."

Zander reached into his pocket and pulled out his wallet. Inside was the required reserves only select status Cupids carried. Five hundred dollars in cash. A pre-paid two-thousand-dollar Visa card—just in case an assignment required an overnight stay or longer on Earth. In the last six months, Zander checked into a hotel three times, each for a single night.

He got out a fifty. Holding the glass in one hand, he glanced at his heart emblem. Half red. He checked his pockets for the extra vials of magical dust. Where were they?

While Cupid-sized, his magic would last indefinitely … there's no need to panic.

Except … in human form, his magic would probably be gone by tomorrow afternoon. No worries. He had plenty of time to party, catch the first rays of light, transform into a Cupid, and ascend to his realm.

With his plan set, he found an empty table near the back. He stared at the head of a deer mounted on the wall.

Poor creature.

Taking a seat under the buck's head, he sipped his brandy as country music twanged from speakers on the wall. A group of cowboys played pool in the corner. Mostly men sat at the bar.

At a table to his right, an older woman with pink-streaked hair turned her chair. "Hi." She seemed sweet and harmless.

"Hello."

"We're about to start our special version of blackjack. Loser buys the next round of shooters. Come join us," the gray-haired lady next to her said.

"Why not?" He had nothing else to do. "I'm Zander." He shook hands with both women and sat next to pinky.

"Nice to meet you." The pink-haired lady shuffled and dealt the first card to each of them face up. He had an ace. Not bad. Pinky got a queen, gray-haired a seven. Dealt his second card, he got a three. Well, at least the ace could count as one or eleven.

"Hit me," he said and received a ten. Making his hand

worth fourteen points. Anything more than a seven, and he'd lose. Still, he said, "Hit me." He got a queen and groaned. Pinky had a jack and king. Gray-haired a seven and ten.

A waitress stopped by their table.

"The round's on him. What are you buying us?" Pink said with a grin.

"Three Buttery Nipples, please."

Pinky laughed. "What's in a buttery nipple?"

"Bacardi and Wild Turkey. Started drinking it in college."

"I'll have to share this drink with my daughter." Gray-haired winked. She lost the next round and ordered Kamikazes."

"You ladies are wicked."

"Don't you forget it. Might as well start on our next hand. Hottie, you get to deal." Gray-haired handed him the cards.

"Drink up folks," Gray-hair said.

He downed the potent limed-flavored concoction. "Hits the spot." The games continued; shots kept coming.

"Why's a handsome lad like you all alone?" Pinky asked as she dealt cards.

"Girl trouble." Feeling a bit muddled, he wanted to forget what happened to him.

The waitress handed them a Red-Headed Slut. Gray-hair's choice. He slammed it down.

"A perfect remedy for your troubles," Pinky said.

"Sure is," he slurred. He'd lost track of how many rounds he bought, much less how many shots he'd downed. Handed another drink, he drank it.

The door opened. A woman strutted in with a dark-haired man. Blonde hair spiraled to her waist. Both sat at the bar.

"Cami?"

"Something wrong?" one of the women asked.

"My ex just walked in." Cami should be with *him* and not that loser. "Excuse me, ladies."

He stood and tapped the man on the shoulder. "You stole my fiancé."

"Are you talking to me?" The man turned.

Zander lifted his elbow back, aimed for the jerk's jaw. The momentum caused Zander's fist to slam into the hard wooden bar, and he stumbled into the guy knocking him off his stool.

"What the hell do you think you're doing?" The guy grabbed Zander behind his arms.

Zander caught his breath and stared at the woman. "Shit. You're not Cami."

"You're drunk. A night in jail aughta sober you up." The guy said and clicked metal cuffs around his wrists. "These keep you from hurting yourself or anyone else. Randy, call the station and send for a car."

"Sure. Thanks for helping out on your night off."

Zander couldn't tell who talked or exactly what was happening.

"No problem," somebody said, nudging him forward, pushed him outside and into the back of a police car. "What the hell?"

CHAPTER 3

Moosehead, Idaho
Population 4,213

Situated in the southern part of Idaho, the resort town of Moosehead had its charm. From Ivelisse Venturi's office window, she had a view of Moosehead Lake. Specks of people canoed, kayaked, paddle boarded, water skied, and swam. One of these days, she'd get out of the office and go out on the lake—one of these days.

After finishing college, she came here to get a fresh start while she worked on her law degree. This paralegal job in a small tourist town had been a godsend. People waved and several called her by her given name. Here, she found peace.

The office secretary, Gladys Meddleton, buzzed the intercom to say her last appointment for the day had arrived. Ivy slipped on her pointy pumps from under her desk, tugged the hemline of her pencil skirt down to cover her knees, and buttoned the matching magenta jacket. She closed her eyes, took a deep calming breath and told Gladys to send in the divorce consultation. Her boss trusted her to interview the client and discuss the dissolution process. If Firebrand Law took on this case, she would be in charge of doing most of the legwork including filing the legal documents.

The door opened, and a frazzled woman with two toddlers in tow marched in. Twins dressed in matching sailor suits, their red hair sticking up, their faces lit with mischievous grins. Whatever went on with the parents didn't appear to affect them.

Ivy picked up two stuffed tigers from the toy box and kneeled down to their level. "Would you like to play with these?"

"Yes," one said. The other nodded and sat on the floor near the couch.

Ivy smiled at the woman. After witnessing her mother's five divorces firsthand, she'd decided a long time ago she'd never have children. Custody battles were her least favorite cases. Children usually got the brunt end of the deal. She knew this from personal experience.

"Thanks for seeing me on such short notice," the woman said and plunked into the seat across from Ivy.

Ivy opened up a file on the computer.

"My husband's having an affair." Tears formed in her eyes.

Ivy pushed her a box of Kleenex. "Adultery cases are

costly and difficult to prove. Most people choose no-fault divorce."

"My husband's not going to like it. He's threatened to take the kids if I ever left him, but I couldn't stay with him another day."

Ivy had seen the husband around town. He owned several business offices, including one near the waterfront. The man reminded Ivy of her mother's third husband, the one who never left a mark on her but demeaned her behind closed doors, calling her stupid and useless. The potential client in front of her had been smart to get away from him, but Ivy doubted the case would be easy.

"Where are you currently residing?"

"With my mother. She has a two-bedroom condo."

At least the woman had a place to go, unlike her mom who had taken Ivy and her siblings to an abused women's shelter. Her stomach clenched. "Has he ever been abusive?"

The woman's head dropped. "Um, I don't care to comment." The toddlers' coos erupted in squeals. The woman called, "Come over here," and the boys crawled into her lap.

"They're adorable," Ivy said.

The woman hugged both boys. "How long will the divorce take?"

"The dissolution can be completed in about six weeks, but if there's a custody battle and trouble splitting property ..." Ivy paused.

"This one isn't going to be easy." The woman gave a half-hearted smile.

Twenty minutes later, Ivy had a signed contract on her desk. She took off her suit jacket and skirt and hung it in the closet, changing into jeans, a T-shirt, and Etnie skate shoes. She picked up her skateboard stashed under her desk. Paralegal by day, radical by night.

Adding a baseball cap worn backward, she headed out the door and glided toward the Blue Birch Cafe around the corner, dodging an older couple. She loved the summertime weather in Moosehead. The crisp mountain air smelled of pine trees.

Reaching the door, she flipped her board into her hand and spotted her friend Sammy waving at her from a booth along the wall of windows. "Long day, huh?"

Ivy settled into the opposite bench. "Another problematic divorce case."

Her friend rolled her large blue eyes.

"At least my boss doesn't take criminal cases." The lawyer on the fifth floor handled those clients. Her office represented probate, wills, business issues, divorces, and various civil cases.

Sammy picked up her menu. "Wanna share a Cobb salad?"

"Only if we get a bottle of Chardonnay to go with it."

"As if you need to ask."

CHAPTER 4

"Hello," an unfamiliar man's voice reverberated through Zander's brain. Where in Hades was he?

Prying open his eyes, his temples throbbed. He focused on the bars surrounding him. More bars on the side separated him from the empty room to his left. Holy Zeus. He'd landed in an Earthly jail. Locked inside a six-by-nine-foot cubicle.

He sucked in several deep breaths. The stench of disinfectant made his stomach lurch. He dashed for the toilet in the back corner and retched. How much did he drink last night? Using the top of the seat to help him rise, he stared at his reflection in a polished metal mirror.

Bloodshot eyes.

Pale face.

Hair in disarray.

Turning on the faucet, he cupped his hands to get water, swished the liquid in his mouth, and spit it out.

Those nice old ladies at the bar encouraged him to drink —not that it took much coercion to get inebriated. Last night, he'd needed to forget. Today, he couldn't stand looking at himself. Some golden boy he turned out to be. The fact that he and his father, grandfather, great grandfather, several aunts and uncles, two older brothers, and countless cousins were all Cupid archers made their family a legend. His ability surpassed every one of them—which didn't matter in the least here on Earth.

He took two steps, dropped to the edge of the cot, and flicked his fingertips to make a hangover concoction. Not even a teeny smidgeon of dust appeared.

Why isn't it working?

He tried his fingertips again.

Nothing.

He shook his hands, rotated his wrists, slammed them on the bed.

Nothing.

He traced his heart emblem on his wrist. Typically, a ruby red color, it had faded to white. Consuming all that alcohol must have depleted his magic.

He felt inside his pants pockets for the vials of magical dust kept for emergencies.

Empty.

Right. He couldn't find any dust last night when he checked.

"Holy Shit." Before he left home, he hadn't followed the usual protocol to create four vials—meaning he was royally screwed. His aching discolored fist proved he'd acted really stupid. He vaguely remembered trying to punch someone. Must be why he got arrested. Footsteps sounded in the hall.

A man in a black uniform with a shiny badge strutted to the front of the bars. "How's your head this morning?" the officer snickered.

"Been better."

"What made you get so drunk?"

"My ex got married yesterday." Zander shook his head.

"And you figured you could drink away your worries?"

"Not one of my better decisions. I mean, on occasion I have a drink or two but getting plastered is not my style. Believe me, I learned my lesson."

"I certainly hope so." The cop squinted at him.

"When will you let me out?" Zander despised confined spaces.

"Once you sign your ticket with the clerk out front, you'll be released on your own recognizance," the cop said. "Your arraignment date will be written at the top. Be warned if you don't return to see the judge, there'll be a warrant for your arrest." Keys jingled, the lock clinked, and the barred door squeaked open. "With both public intoxication and disturbing the peace charges against you, I suggest you get a lawyer."

"Know any good ones." In Cupid's Corner, his Eros name would be more than enough to get him out of any dilemma, but he couldn't count on his prestigious connections to mean anything on Earth. Stuck here for the time being, he had no intention of spending another minute in a jail cell.

"As a matter of fact, yes, I do." The officer unlocked the door, reached into his shirt pocket, and handed Zander a card. "Take a right on Cardinal Way and a left on Hemlock Avenue. His office is on the fifth floor in the only brick building on the street."

"Thanks."

The cop led him to a woman with thick black glasses behind the counter. "Robin will be helping you."

"What brings you to Moosehead, Mr. Eros?" the clerk asked.

"Needed a vacation." Zander signed the document in plain black ink. His signature lacked the usual pizazz of glittery ruby shimmer. Appearance date: July 2nd.

30 days from now.

He went outside, breathed in the fresh air and strategized his next moves.

Food. Change of clothes. Shower. Place to stay.

He could do this.

CHAPTER 5

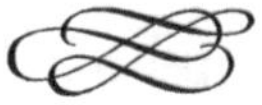

The street inclined slightly, giving Zander a spectacular view of a lake about three blocks away. Paddle boarders and kayakers shared the space with sailboats and speedboats. People sunbathed along the sandy shoreline. This place reminded him of summers spent at Lake Aphrodite.

Two women in short-shorts and skin-tight tank tops approached him. "Hey," one woman said.

He gave them an acknowledgment nod, wishing he showered so he didn't feel grungy.

A shop's sign hung from the awning. *Possibilities*. Interesting word. For as long as he could recall, his life had been planned and organized by others. Here in Moosehead, he could choose what to do next—the idea was both freeing and terrifying.

A Porsche drove down the street. He'd driven a flashy sports car during his last visit on Earth. Why hadn't he created one for this trip? Alcohol had not been his friend.

He passed Deer in the Headlights Bookstore. Catchy name. Another block and he came to Moosehead Burgers, the aroma making his stomach growl. He walked inside and stared at the menu on a whiteboard.

Elk burger. Moose burger. Turkey burger.

No thanks.

Grilled cheese sandwich.

Score! He strode up to the counter.

"May I help you?" a pimply-faced teen asked.

"Grilled cheese, fries, and a strawberry Fantasy."

The teen tilted his head. "That'll be ten-fifty-seven."

Zander slid a fifty across the counter.

The teen held it up to the light and checked the bill.

A lump formed in the back of his throat. The money had been created using magic. With his luck, he'd get arrested for counterfeiting. The clerk handed him his change and gave a plastic marker with the number thirteen, Zander chose a table at the side of the room.

Now what?

If only he'd been assigned to a big city. It'd be easier to find a Cupid archer on assignment and get him or her to assist him to return home. It could be months, even years before someone else from his realm spotted him in a rural setting.

Years without the comforts of his celestial realm?

He released his breath. Somebody would notice his assignments weren't completed this week and trace his last location to Moosehead.

No, they wouldn't. He cleared his June calendar.

Holy Shit. How would anyone find him? The critical factor in locating a Cupid—magic.

Actually, not being able to pinpoint him was to his advantage. Still, he really should clear his name for future visits. That way his mishap while in human form wouldn't be discovered. At least he hoped his reasoning worked.

He rolled his shoulders and smiled. No one knew him in Moosehead. There were no expectations. He could become someone different. Create a different identity for the next month. Have some fun.

Rockabilly music came from speakers on the wall. Tolerable, but he preferred rock and roll. The teen delivered his food. Zander devoured his cheese sandwich in about four bites and wished he'd ordered two. He dipped his fries in ketchup and guzzled his slushy. The cold gave him a brain freeze.

Now to find a change of clothes. Get a room. Shower. Sleep.

He counted out his money. Three-hundred-sixty-five dollars plus almost two thousand on his pre-paid Visa should hold him a few weeks.

Leaving the building, he strolled toward the shoreline and spotted a skateboard shop on the other side of the street.

While in college, he and his friends skateboarded around town.

He crossed the street, his heart thumping in a fast, happy beat. Walking inside, the smell of gear oil and grip tape adhesive reminded him of helping out in a shop his friend's dad owned. He'd learned to build and fix boards the non-magical way. A red and black SK8DLX board drew him to the wall display. He ran his hand along the surface.

"That one makes a great trick board." A freckle-faced clerk handed it to him.

Zander spun the wheels and noticed the two-hundred-dollar sticker. "That's out of my budget."

"Got a couple of rebuilt ones in the back if you'd like to look."

"No thanks." With limited resources and no clue how much a hotel room would cost, he'd better be careful with his money, or he'd soon be sleeping outside on the hard ground. Not a good option for a Cupid used to snoozing on a cloud-soft bed.

"You know of any decently-priced hotels?"

"The Big Moose Motel's the cheapest, but it's close to the interstate. There's a couple of others on the outskirts of town. If you want something close to the lake, I'd stay at the Moosehead Lodge."

The Moosehead Lodge's close vicinity to that bar made it far from desirable.

"You might chance finding a cabin at the Moosehead State Park." The clerk pulled out a brochure.

"Any idea where I can get a phone?" Zander shrugged. "Somehow, I lost mine."

"There's a shop next to the market on Lakeshore Drive."

He opened the brochure. Two hundred a week for a single cabin.

Perfect.

CHAPTER 6

Tuesday morning

Not about to miss his meeting with the lawyer, Zander sprinted down the campground's gravelly road toward the summer trolley stop. Stuck in this town for who knows how long, he had to find out the consequences for his public intoxication and disturbing the peace charges. Since he never ever wanted to return to a dreadful jail cell, hopefully, hiring a lawyer wouldn't cost much.

At the trolley stop, a young couple and their two children waited on a bench in the shade.

The woman bounced an infant on her lap. "I believe your cabin's next to ours."

"It is." The cherubs wailing had echoed through the thin walls, keeping Zander up most of the night. He shouldn't complain. Somebody had canceled their four-week reservation, giving him a bed and a place to shower. However, the accommodations lacked any luxuries whatsoever. He was used to his spacious apartment with a separate dining, living, and bedroom. He was used to sleeping on a cloud-soft bed. He was used to creating food at the flick of his fingertips. As a prestigious archer family, he lived a pampered life. A bug buzzed near his ear and flew off, only to return a few seconds later. He swatted at the pesky insect and missed.

"We're off for the beach," the man said, holding a toddler.

Zander would much rather be out on the water, but he had to meet with the attorney, so he pulled out the business card from his pocket to double-check the street.

An enormous green trolley rumbled to a halt in front of the sign. Zander followed the family inside and took a seat behind the driver. "How long before we stop at Hemlock Street?"

"About ten minutes."

If only he had his wings to flutter around town. Instead, he stared out the window as the vehicle passed a coffee shop, antique stores, and various buildings scattered between vacant lots.

"Next stop, Moosehead Way. If you're staying at the Lodge, this is you," the driver shouted.

His assignment at Moosehead Lodge had gone off flawlessly. Walking across the street led to his fiasco. His gut twisted.

At the next stop, an assortment of people piled onto the trolley. Two men in business suits carried briefcases. An obvious vacationer wore a bright yellow Hawaiian shirt. A large family boarded carrying towels and backpacks.

"Is this seat taken?" A middle-aged man with glasses and tattered jeans patched in several spots asked him.

"No."

The guy scooted next to Zander so close he could smell cigarette smoke on his clothing.

The engine made a grinding noise, and the vehicle lurched forward. Zander hit his knee on the driver's seat and sucked in a groan.

"You from around here?" the man next to him asked.

"No. Just vacationing."

"Me too. Where are you staying?"

Humans sure could be nosey. "A cabin at the state park."

"Had my honeymoon there." The man gave a wistful sigh. "Oh, to be young and in love again."

Until the girl runs off with a mortal. He let out a long sigh. Time to let go of his aggravation over his ex.

CHAPTER 7

Zander compared the address on the brick building with the card. 1222. That's it. He entered the empty lobby. Did he really need a lawyer? After all, he might be home within the month. What if no one bothers to trace him here? A shiver shuddered up his spine.

The rubber soles on his sandals squeaked as he moved toward the elevator. It dinged and opened. He glanced inside the metal box. Not in a million years would he step in there. An arrow with the word "stairs" pointed north, and he quickly made it to the bottom. Inching to unfurl his wings, this would be a breeze to fly up. Holy Aphrodite, he missed magic.

He ran up the four flights of stairs. At least his regiment at the gym had paid off. He walked to the landing.

Firebrand Law Offices.

The name made him chuckle. Was this the place? He plucked the card from his pocket. Nope.

Jim Brown LLP. Criminal Law. Suite 505.

He trotted up one more flight, strolled inside the men's restroom, peered into a mirror above the sink, and combed his hair with his fingers. Presentable.

A clock on the wall showed he had ten minutes to spare.

He found the law office at the end of a long corridor on the left and went inside. Tall windows lit the room. High ceilings gave the office an airy feel. He went up to a desk with a glass top. A stocky man who seemed about Zander's age smiled. "May I help you?"

"I have an appointment with Jim Brown."

"Have a seat and fill out these papers." He handed him a clipboard. "I'll let him know you've arrived."

He sat at a plaid loveseat near the windows. The form asked for his last residence. He pulled out his Cupid-created ID and copied it. For employment, he put in the information he had for Heavenly Valley Custom Arrows.

"Mr. Brown will see you now."

He went inside the open office. A middle-aged man with black spectacles took his clipboard and typed his info into his computer.

"Thank you for meeting with me." He extended his hand, and they shook.

"You were arrested for public intoxication and disturbing the peace. What is your rendition of the events?"

"Had a little too much to drink."

The lawyer gave him a no-nonsense look. "Care to elaborate?"

"Well … I got plastered. Not one of my finer moments, but … to be fair … my ex got married Saturday." He swallowed hard.

"And?" He folded his arms and waited. "I assume there is more."

It was as if he read minds.

"Okay," he cleared his throat. "First of all, I don't usually get drunk. I mean, maybe I have a few drinks, but that's it."

"The more you can tell me about what happened, the better I can represent you."

"Umm … I started playing cards with these nice old ladies. Tourists from what they said." Holy Hades, his throat felt dry. He could use water, but the serious expression on the lawyer's face said he'd better not ask for a drink. "Anyway, the losing hand bought the next round of shots."

"About how many shots did you have?"

"Well … I lost count." He shrugged.

"Is that all that happened?" His shoulders stiffened as he eyed him.

"The door opened … and this cowboy walked in with a woman that looked just like my ex … and I took a swing at him and hit the bar. Next thing I know, I was handcuffed and placed in the backseat of a cop car. After that, everything was pretty much a blur."

"Thanks for the specific details. That gives me a clearer picture of your case." The lawyer sat a little straighter and glanced at his computer. "I see you were released under your own recognizance."

"I just made a monumental mistake. One I never plan on repeating again."

"Do you have any other violations?" He didn't look up as he typed.

"Got a speeding ticket as a teen." He got a speeding ticket for flying too fast on a Cupid's Corner street.

"Why do you believe you need representation?"

"One night in a jail cell is more than enough."

"Public intoxication and disturbing the peace may result in a hefty fine and possible local jail time. But seeing as you have no record, the magistrate may lean towards community service and a monetary reparation."

"May? That's not acceptable. My family will clip my wings if the Eros reputation is tarnished." He fiddled with his shirt's button.

"Interesting vernacular." The lawyer squinted at him as if he were the odd one here.

"I need this incident to be cleared off my record." If word got out in Cupid's Corner that he'd been acting like a human and arrested in a public bar, who knows what might happen to him?

"No relative has ever been arrested?"

"None that I've ever met." He shook his head.

"If I choose to represent you, I will fight to get your charges dropped."

"If?" How could this lawyer not represent him? "What

will it take? Money? A couple of phone calls to the right person?"

"Not with this judge. He's by the book. But fair. Your arraignment is in 29 days. How long do you plan on staying in town?"

"A month. Possibly two." He wished the stupid arrest never happened. But it did. "I'm on a much-deserved vacation."

He took off his glasses and spun them. "It's six-hundred dollars to represent you. More if there are any complications that arise. I required three hundred down. The balanced paid when the case is concluded."

This would take a big chunk out of his living expenses. If he were here longer than a week, he'd need to find a job. "You take credit cards?" He pulled out his wallet.

"Absolutely."

The lawyer printed a document. "Sign and hand this form to my secretary. He'll take care of the credit transaction at his desk."

"Thanks for taking me on." He offered his hand and gave him a firm handshake.

A few minutes later, he stood on the corner of Cardinal Way and Hemlock Avenue waiting for a car to pass.

A woman zipped up next to him. Her luxurious dark braid threaded through the opening in the back of her cap. She flipped a bright pink skateboard in her hand. "Hi," she said.

"Hi. Nice board."

She lowered her sunglasses to chocolate-colored eyes. "Do you skate?"

"Yep."

She flashed him a smile.

The car passed. Her hand brushed his arm as she dropped her board. Hot sparks shot through his body. He sucked in several breaths as he watched her roll across the street, giving him a nice view of her tiny waist and jean-clad backside. He willed himself to be in control. No way could he be attracted to a human.

CHAPTER 8

Wednesday morning, Zander jogged down a sloping trail. Insects buzzed. Music blared from a tent. A thirtyish-looking couple cooked eggs and bacon over a crackling fire pit. Smoke mixed with a fresh pine scent. Birds chirped.

The lake came into view. Water lapped along the shore. A pair of dragonflies skimmed along the water's edge, and he thought about Cami. Dragonflies were drawn to her like he had been as a young boy. He was the perfect choice for her. They could have raised perfect cherubs and lived the perfect life. That Cupid had some nerve dumping him.

Then an image of that dark-haired woman on the skateboard came to mind. Pretty—for a human. Not that he was into humans.

He stopped, picked up a stone and skipped it along the

water. All his life, he'd been told you can't change fate. His assignment sent him to the Moosehead Lodge—however, he chose to enter the Bison Tavern all on his own. The blame for his stint on Earth—himself. But he would survive.

He went back to his cabin about the size of a closet. He'd gotten little sleep on a lumpy single mattress. Not the right way to begin this day.

Without a wardrobe to hang his clothing, he used a battered dresser pushed against the wall. Snatching clean clothes he'd purchased at the local discount store, he settled for a T-shirt and Khaki shorts. Nothing designer. Nothing expensive. Never again would he take the ability to create clothing with the flick of magical dust for granted.

He had time to kill. What to do?

Swim.

He'd forgotten to buy trunks. Forced to use the mortal's monetary system, his funds were dwindling. He'd overheard the lady who ran the campground mention to one of the vacationers about a thrift shop that had some quality stuff.

Why not give it a try?

An hour later, he got off the trolley at Elderberry Street and stepped up on the curb. A truck barreled past. Holy Hades. The vehicle could have hit him.

He passed a bright red building with dark green shutters and a wooden door carved with a moose knocker. This town seemed to have a strange obsession with animal artifacts. An enormous man with barrel-sized arms held two banker-sized boxes from the back of a pickup. He pointed to Zander. "Sir. Think you could give me a hand with these boxes?"

Zander looked behind him. No one there.

"Please."

"You want my help?" He didn't get why this stranger asked him.

"I'd really appreciate it." The massive guy had a bald head and a scary stare. "Now."

It wasn't as if he could furl his wings and fly off. Besides, he wasn't pressed for time, and no telling how long he'd be stuck in this town. Plus, he might need an ally in the future. "Okay." He lifted a box. "What's in here, rocks?"

The guy let out a loud guffaw. "Donations. Mostly canned food."

He followed the man to the side of the building and into a warehouse.

"I help out with the Moosehead food bank when I'm not busy running my business. People come here when they're down on their luck."

If Zander hadn't brought that pre-paid Visa, he would be accepting charity from this place. Unheard of. The Eros' family founded charities.

He placed the boxes on the ground at the side of the room. Shelving lined the sides of the open-beamed space. A variety of canned foods were neatly stacked. Long tables lined the center as a few people filled boxes. A warehouse of supplies for the needy.

"Name's Brutus." The guy held out his hand.

"Zander." If this guy squeezed any tighter, Zander's fingers would break. "I'd be happy to help you load up the rest of those boxes."

"Be obliged. Better grab a dolly." The big guy motioned to a big metal thing with wheels.

For the next few hours, Zander stacked boxes, unpacked them, and organized the shelves. His biceps ached after the strenuous workout.

"Mind mopping the floor?" Brutus asked.

Zander didn't have a clue how to do that, nor did he care to learn. "Not today. I better get going."

"It was worth a try." The guy lifted a shoulder. "As you can see, we're always short-handed. Feel free to stop by here anytime."

"I might do that." He continued south about half a block. The thrift shop doors were propped open, allowing him to wander inside. Think of this as an adventure. Pretend to be an explorer looking for a big discovery. The thought made him smile.

He zeroed in on the men's clothing racks, passed the pants, and slowed at the shorts. Arranged by sizes, he sifted through the thirty-fours and checked a pair of beige shorts with a tear in the crotch. No thanks. Then he pulled out a pair of black cargo shorts that appeared fairly new. He examined them. They smelled like laundry detergent. Five dollars. They'd do.

The swim trunks were on the next aisle over. He searched and found a pair of Quicksilver with the original tag. Ten dollars—a steal.

A banner waved above the front counter—50% off all clothing. He found three relatively new T-shirts. If his family could see him now. He couldn't help chuckling.

As ironic as it had been being sent to the romantic location of Moosehead Lake, he decided the place had its charm.

He walked past a row of bicycles. If he rode a bike around town, he could avoid the bus. A bin on the ground seemed to call out to him. He picked up a bicycle pump, a pair of tiny fins, and a skateboard. The top looked a bit worn but still rideable. Two wheels spun out of balance. Easy fix. He recalled his college days. He'd broken the trucks on his board. His friend dared him to learn to fix it without magic. Zander couldn't refuse a dare and ended up spending time at the shop his friend's dad owned.

Unlike the Eros family, some Cupids proved they could complete tasks without magic. In his college town of Lover's Landing, there had been a market for do-it-yourselfers while folks in Cupid's Corner scoffed at such a thing.

Thanks to his friend's dare, he could handle this. All he had to do was buy some bearings at the skate shop. The price on the bottom read $9.99. Yep, he'd get this. He stood on the board and rode it down the aisle.

He spent less than twenty dollars at the store, took the

trolley to Caribou Avenue, and got off. The board shop had a help wanted sign in the window.

The same freckle-faced clerk greeted him. "See you found a board."

"Needs bearings. Thought I'd try ABEC 7."

The clerk took the board and spun the wheels. "Good choice. Got a set on sale for ten dollars."

The same price as he'd paid for the board.

"I can install them for an extra five."

"Think I could borrow some tools and do it myself?"

"Sure. Follow me to the back." He brought Zander to a workbench with boards, grip tape, hardware, and miscellaneous items haphazardly spread on the table.

"Help yourself." The door beeped, announcing a customer, and the clerk left.

Zander used a ratchet to remove the wheels and carefully pry off the bearings. He did the same for the other three wheels. In no time, he had the bearings replaced and the wheels back on.

"You're done already," the clerk asked and checked his work. "Nice."

"Saw your help wanted sign in the window. I'll take the job."

"Not up to me. You gotta fill out this form. I'll give it to my boss."

Really? They expected *him* to fill out an application. How quaint. He took the clipboard and sat at the bench.

CHAPTER 9

At three-thirty on Friday, Ivy skated toward the Caribou Board Shop to check out shoes. Unlike her girlfriends who preferred fancy purses or designer heels, she craved the smell of leather on a new pair of DC's or Osiris' or Etnies'. She loved the feel of their padded heels and appreciated soles that gripped the board perfectly. Currently owning dozens of styles, her favorite pink pair were getting pretty ratty. Great excuse to indulge her inner skater. If a new outfit and another board happened to roll its way into the deal, so be it. She could afford to splurge on herself every once in a while.

Ivy's passion for skating started at age ten. Her mother's husband—number four—found a board at a yard sale. She discovered a way to escape from her younger siblings. Husband number four had been Ivy's favorite stepdad.

Unfortunately, that marriage lasted less than two years. The union created her half-sister, Goldie. Ivy still kept in touch with this stepdad.

She went inside the shop heading straight for the shoes at the back and plowed into a solid chest. A man steadied her with muscular arms. She practically drowned in blue eyes that made the sky pale in comparison. As if in a trance, she found herself unable to move, unable to speak, her pulse speeding out of control.

"Are you all right?" he said with a deep timber in his voice.

"S-sorry." She stepped back and recognized the blond guy with a long crew cut. It dawned on her she was gawking at the man she'd sort of met him at the corner where she worked. But that had been a quick blip. Right now, she'd describe him as Hunky. Charismatic. Probably Trouble.

"No prob." He flashed her a dazzling white smile.

Her heart whomped in her chest. Ridiculous. She knew firsthand, handsome guys spelled heartache.

"Is there something I could assist you with?" His blue eyes met hers. She'd swear an electric charge arced back and forth between them.

Her friends were right. She needed to date more. Maybe even have a summer fling. "I'm just browsing." Walking to the back of the store, she concentrated on the women's shoes. A purple pair of high tops might work, but she had her heart set on pink.

"Hey." Penelope, her twenty-something friend and

manager of the store, walked in from the stockroom carrying hot pink Diamonds. "Check these out. Got size six in the back if you're interested."

Ivy sat at a cushioned chair and crossed her legs. "Definitely." Joy soared through her.

"I see you've met Zander. He's vacationing for a month or two and thought working here might be a interesting way to pick up some extra cash."

"I hope you checked his background." Her friend didn't always follow protocol.

"I'm working on it." Penelope looked away. "Anyway, he's easy on the eyes."

That's an understatement.

"Zander." Penelope motioned to him. "Let me show you how we organize our stock, and you can grab Ivy's shoes."

Ivy strove to keep her eyes on the shoes or the floor or anywhere other than Zander. Her endeavor lasted for maybe five seconds as he entered the curtained area.

What's up with her? He's just another handsome man. She took off her shoes, leaving on gray and pink striped ankle socks.

Penelope came back. "Zander will be right out with those shoes. I'll be upfront restocking if you need me."

Zander knelt in front of her and took out the shoes.

Hot pink with beige soles, the plain white laces made the perfect accent. The sight of those shoes brought on a conditioned euphoric response. Who needed a man when there were shoes like this?

"Allow me to assist you?" He slipped on the shoe reminding her of Cinderella and her glass slipper. The shoe fit perfectly. Zander tied the laces then slid on the other shoe.

She walked to a long mirror and admired the look. "I'll take them."

"There's a board with the same color." He stepped next to her. "I know how you women love matching things."

"So do most men." She pointed to his navy polo and beige shoes with matching navy laces.

"Guilty." He shrugged.

At the front counter, Ivy took out her credit card. In this shop, money bought happiness.

ZANDER RANG up Ivy's purchases. She didn't flinch at spending over three-hundred dollars. To be honest, if Zander had cash to blow, he'd probably do the same. "You got plans for tomorrow?" His attraction to this woman was strong, and the words just tumbled out.

"Not really." She flipped her waist-long braid behind her shoulder.

Talk about smoking hot—for a human.

"Since I'm off, thought I might try paddle boarding. Know of any good places?" During his trolley rides to town, he spotted paddle boarders on the lake. Now that he'd gotten situated, he wanted to attempt the sport.

"You can get rentals at the marina on Lynch Street and Lakeshore."

"That's not far from the cabin I'm renting. I'm heading out there tomorrow around eleven. Why don't you join me?"

"I'll consider it."

"It's not a date. I don't know many people in town and would like some company."

"Mind if I ask Penelope and some others to join?" One side of her mouth quirked up.

"Not at all." Although, he'd rather have Ivy alone. "It's getting busy. Hope to see you out there."

She walked out the door, and he watched her hips sway.

He unlocked a case and assisted three women looking for sunglasses. People kept coming in. A teenager purchased swim trunks and flip-flops. Another bought a new board. He rang up countless T-shirts, shorts, shoes, bathing suits, swim trunks, wallets, and other items.

Working here didn't follow his archer profession, but he found the job a nice change of pace.

CHAPTER 10

Zander pushed his mirrored sunglasses to the top of his head and strolled up to the marina carrying a backpack with a change of clothes and an oversized towel. Usually cool and confident, he couldn't seem to shake this odd sensation inside his gut.

"May I help you?" A redheaded clerk in a turquoise marina rental shirt asked.

"I'd like to rent a paddle board."

"That'll be forty, plus a hundred for a deposit."

After paying for the cabin, buying clothes, food, along with the lawyer fee, his Visa had only four hundred left. Good thing next week, he'd get paid.

"You've done this before?"

"Nope." Zander doubted it'd be difficult.

"It's like skateboarding with a paddle."

"Sounds fun."

"Put your things in one of the lockers and hang your towel on the rack outside. As a first-time renter, you get one free lesson. When my co-worker comes, I'll take you out and show you the basics."

He couldn't wait to be on the water.

"Help yourself to sunscreen. The rays can be pretty brutal on the lake."

He took off his T-shirt, placed his things inside a locker, shut the door, pulled out the number 7 key, and twirled it on his finger. Then he went outside, snagged a bottle of sunscreen on top of the towel rack, sprayed some on his body, and followed a woman in shorts and a turquoise shirt back into the shop.

"Alexander is a newbie. I'm gonna get him started," the redhead said.

"It's Zander." His father went by Alexander.

"Have a good time out there." The brunette waved them on.

The redhead tossed him a bright orange life vest, grabbed a neon green and white board from the ones stacked vertically in groves, and handed him a tall board.

He dropped his sunglasses in place, walked next to the clerk toward the shore on the other side of the boat dock, held his longboard perpendicular, and paddle under his arm. The rocky shore crunched under his strapped-on sandals as he waded into the murky gray, green water.

"Once you're up to your waist, position yourself on your knees."

He hopped on with ease.

"Hold one hand on the paddle's top and the other on the shaft," she said. "Get comfortable with your oar."

He moved forward a few yards in the water. Easy.

"Stand slowly, keeping to the middle, feet parallel, knees slightly bent." She demonstrated.

Using his knees, he rose to two feet and tried to steady his position. "Like this?"

"Keep your core centered. Take a few strokes on each side with your oar."

This was entertaining. Toward the middle of the lake, motorboats zipped across the water. To his left people gathered on blankets or under umbrellas along the roped-off shoreline.

"Turning's not hard. Lean your torso in the direction you want to go and place the paddle on that side.

"Got it." The wind whipped his hair across his forehead.

"Hey, Zander." He recognized Ivy's voice and turned his head as she entered the water. His balance shifted. To avoid falling, he dropped to his knees.

"You okay?" the redhead asked.

"Fine." He gulped in several deep breaths and pushed back to his feet.

The clerk maneuvered her board to face the shore. "Finally decided to come out, huh."

"I did." Ivy paddled closer. Her one-piece bathing suit

accentuated her curvy body. Sunlight shone on her dark hair pulled back in a ponytail.

"You know Zander," the clerk asked.

"We've met. He works at Caribou."

"Cool. Well, gotta get back to work, but you two enjoy yourselves." She left, leaving him alone with Ivy.

CHAPTER 11

"Have you done this before?" Zander paddled a little closer to Ivy.

"A few times. And you." Her voice came out tight, controlled.

"First timer." Lame, his tongue seemed to tie.

"Let's head west. There's a cool cove that way."

"Sure." Moving away from the sandy beach, he admired how easily she maneuvered through the water.

"It's pretty far. You up to it?"

"Is that a challenge?" He couldn't help grinning.

"Not at all." She paddled faster.

Yep, this had to be a test. Overhead, a V of geese honked. A fish jumped out of the water. The lake glistened.

"The weather's perfect." She zipped ahead of him.

Focused on her tanned legs and curvy butt, he wobbled

and managed to correct his balance. When he caught up to her, he used his paddle to splash her.

"Hey." She leaned over to get good leverage on her paddle and tumbled into the water.

"You okay?" He felt bad and offered his oar and helped her up.

"Fine." The corners of her mouth quirked up. "The water's refreshing. You should try it."

"Probably will, later." He glanced at her. Water drenched her hair and her toned body.

"We're turning here." She brought her board into an inlet with him right behind her.

He checked out the sun-worn dock with tied-up boats swaying in the current. A fisherman on the end waved, and he waved back.

She pointed to a small cabin overlooking the lake. "I wouldn't mind living in a cottage like that."

"Where do you live now?"

"A condo not far from my office. It's convenient, but I've always dreamed of seeing the lake from my porch."

"Where do you work?"

"In the building where we first met. I'm a paralegal for Firebrand Law."

He thought about saying he'd seen the sign on the door, but then she might ask what he was doing there. Instead, he asked, "Is that really the company's name?"

"My boss said it was catchy. What do you do, I mean, when you're not working at Caribou's?"

Time for the practiced response. “My family owns a bow and arrow manufacturing company. I do odds and ends there.”

“Okay.” She didn’t sound the least bit impressed. Fine. His job did sound boring.

“What made you become a paralegal?”

“I suppose I could blame my mother. Law has always fascinated me. When I was fifteen, she went through her fourth divorce. I couldn’t help peppering her lawyer with questions. The following summer, he hired me to help out with filing and answering the phones. One day I’ll become a lawyer. Being a paralegal is the next best thing.”

“Four divorces. That must’ve been rough.”

“Actually, she’s had five. Mom has this idiotic notion that one day she’ll find her true love.”

“You don’t believe in love.” Her comment bothered him.

“Why would I? It’s a fallacy that begins with little girls and fairytales about happily ever after.”

“Everyone deserves happiness.”

“I don’t require a Prince Charming to be content.”

Obviously, her freewill to avoid love kicked in strong. Since he didn’t have the ability to help, he splashed her again.

“Are you a hopeless romantic?” She eyed him.

Not at the moment. But the Cupid in him wouldn’t stop hoping to find his soulmate. He focused on a paraglider above the lake’s center. “Next time, I’m trying that,” he shouted.

She turned her head sideways, her rich brown eyes glittering, her mouth rounded. "Watch out for the wake."

His board faltered. He bent his knees, attempting to correct his balance, but found himself plunging into the water in slow motion. A cool liquid surrounded him, his breath stopped, and his eyes blurred. His life vest propelled him to the surface, and he coughed out a mouthful of brackish water.

"You all right?" Ivy held his oar with hers and used it to push his board towards him.

"Yes. I chose to take a swim." His fingers latched onto a smooth epoxy side, and he pulled up onto the deck. Droplets of water rolled down his body.

"Sure you did." Her warm eyes shone with humor.

"Like you said, the water is refreshing."

She glanced at her wristwatch. "It's already been an hour. Let's head back."

He stood with his knees slightly bent for stabilization.

They glided across the water, paddling fast, past a two-seater kayak, people floating on inner tubes, and a pair of rowboats. The air swooshed. Water sprayed from his oar. She moved ahead. He caught up and passed her. In no time, he spotted the shore and then the marina shop.

"Last one in buys lunch." Her oar slid through the water.

No way would he let her show him up.

People bobbed and splashed near the shore as he pushed through the water and caught up to Ivy. He jumped off the board and ran to the beach, beating her by a few seconds. "So, what's for lunch?"

"Meatball sandwiches." She stepped onto the walkway, set her board in a rack outside the shop, and reached for her towel.

He did the same, dried off, and held the door open for Ivy.

"Did you guys enjoy yourselves?" the redheaded clerk asked.

"Absolutely." The sides of Ivy's mouth quirked upward.

"The water's quite refreshing." He grabbed a pair of mirrored sunglasses off the rack, saw the fifty-dollar price tag and put them back. "Thanks for giving me the basics."

"No prob." She handed them their locker keys.

After changing in the shop's dressing room, he waited for Ivy to walk out. She wore shorts and a tank top. Sexy. Not that he was looking. He held the door and walked out with Ivy at his side. "I'm starving. Hope the sandwich shop isn't far."

She flipped her long dark hair behind her. "Up about a block."

Heavenly saints, she was pretty.

THIRTY MINUTES LATER, Ivy and Zander ate their lunches under a tree with a view of the lake. A couple of squirrels skittered up the trunk as if playing their own version of tag. Oh to be that carefree.

Although, she'd settle for more free time.

She sipped her soda and gazed at Zander. His mouth tipped up, showing his dimples, and she could swear her pulse sped up. Her rational side knew to be wary of handsome men like Zander. Too bad her wild side fought to listen. "When did you start skateboarding?" She asked trying to break their silence.

"College. Found it a great alternative to get across campus." He bit into his veggie sandwich. Obviously, a health nut.

"What about you?"

"Fifth grade."

"You must be pretty good."

"I can hold my own." She wasn't about to say she'd dreamed of being in the X Games. That had been a childish illusion. "When I skateboard, it helps me unwind."

"I get it. Skating gives me a sense of freedom. It's like you're flying." He looked off to the distance.

"There are times when I wish I had wings and could fly away." She laughed. "Go ahead and say it, I'm delusional."

"Not at all." She expected him to disagree—not look stone serious.

"This has been a nice day." She dug her foot in the sand. "I forgot how therapeutic water can be."

"Me, too. But I'm on vacation now, so I plan to do a whole lot of relaxing."

"But you're working at Caribou's." Was he broke or had she missed something?

"Had a blast working in a board shop in college. When I saw the help wanted sign, I thought I could earn extra money in case I decide to extend my stay another month or two."

"Have you been to the skate park on Gray Fox yet?"

"No. I'm off at noon on Tuesday, thought I'd try it out. Wanna join me?" Again there came that dimpled grin, the one she struggled to refuse.

"Sorry. I've got to work." Plus, she had a paper due for her class on Wednesday.

"Another time, then?"

"Maybe." Was he asking her out? She wasn't quite sure.

"I know you skateboard and paddle board. What else do you like to do?" His blue eyes twinkled.

"Anything in the water, plus snowboarding and cross-country skiing in the winter. When I was in high school, I used to play soccer." Until her junior year and they moved again. "How 'bout you? I bet you played baseball in high school." She checked out his lean build and long legs. "Wait, make that Lacrosse."

"Nope." He blinked. "Just archery."

"Is that really a sport?" She chuckled. "I mean, it takes skill but not necessarily athletic ability."

Frowning, he folded his arms. "It takes talent to be an expert marksman."

"And you're good?"

"I'm the best."

"And you never brag?" She appreciated his confidence.

"Not about this. I've been shooting since I was a cher-child." He gave her a wry grin.

"What's a cher-child?"

"A kid." He shrugged. "Anyway, I'd be happy to show you sometime. Might even give you some pointers if you like."

"You're on." Her darn words agreed a little too quickly.

CHAPTER 12

Ivy flipped her board up into her hand and rushed inside Carly's Cantina. A mariachi band serenaded a couple near the back. The scent of grilled food had her stomach grumbling. Because of her crazy, busy day, she'd forgotten to eat lunch. Sammy waved at their usual table across from the bar. The place was packed. Taco Tuesday.

"Hey, girls," Ivy said to her friends as she stuffed her cap inside her backpack and placed it alongside her skateboard on the floor.

"Did you enjoy yourself paddle boarding Saturday?" Penelope arched a brow.

"I did. The water was great."

"Sorry I couldn't join you. I'm surprised you went anyway." Penelope tilted her head.

"It's a public place. Besides, you guys have been telling me to get out of the office." This was true enough. They'd also been bugging her to start dating again.

"Who'd you go with? I can't believe that I go out of town for one week and Ivy's dating." Sammy smoothed her blonde hair behind her ear.

"She went with Zander the guy I just hired at the board shop."

"Don't make a big deal out of it. We just happened to be at the same location and purchased our own rentals." Ivy refused to play into their game.

"What's Zander like?" Sammy folded her hands under her chin.

"He's nice enough … for a vacationer." Ivy glanced at the floor not about to say he's hot, sleek, and way too handsome man.

"You're blushing," Penelope said.

"As I told you earlier, I only went because I wanted to get out on the water." Ivy's pulse sped a little faster. No way would she admit she'd dreamt about Zander kissing her. Even now, she wondered if his kisses would be as smoking as his body. "Remember, he's only a clerk."

"That's not true. His family manufactures bows and arrows," Penelope said.

"Then why is he working?" Sammy reached for a tortilla chip and dipped it in salsa.

"His fiancé dumped him, and he had to get out of town."

Ivy had heard that one. How in the heck did Penelope learn that?

"He said he took the job to take his mind off things." Penelope smirked. The girl could pry info from the devil himself.

"He's on the rebound, plus he'll be gone in a month. You'll have to be careful with your heart around him." Sammy stared at her.

"Can we please change topics?" Ivy asked.

"Fine, for now anyway." Sammy giggled.

Thankfully, the waitress walked up. They ordered margaritas with their tacos.

"You'll never guess who just walked in?" Penelope waved at someone behind Ivy.

Ivy didn't bother turning.

"Zander, Rick, come join us," Penelope called.

Rick worked at the ice cream shop next to Caribou Skateboards. He threaded his fingers through his dark wavy hair, grabbed a chair. and scooted in on the end.

"Hello." Zander slid his board under an empty seat and moved in next to her. His eyes met hers. Seriously, it had to be illegal to have such a gorgeous blue color.

"This is Sammy," Penelope said.

"Nice meeting you." Sammy gave a-vibrant smile, not at all acting like Zander had just been the focus of their conversation. "What brings you to Moosehead?"

"Vacation."

"You picked a perfect time to enjoy the lake." Sammy kept her eyes focused on him. "Ivy said you went paddle boarding."

"We did." He glanced over at Ivy, and she shivered.

"You went out with him?" Rick pointed towards Zander. "I've been trying to get her to go out with me for two years."

"It wasn't a date?" She said at the same time as Zander.

The waitress came out with their drinks. Zander ordered a beer. She sipped her margarita and listened to the mariachi band who had moved closer to their table.

"Where you from?" Sammy asked.

"Heavenly Valley."

"Heard snowboarding's rad up there. Doubt it compares to Moosehead Mountain," Penelope said.

"Since I'll be gone before winter, you've just given me a good excuse to come back."

"Dude, it's got some gnarly black diamond trails," Rick added.

Ivy had been so busy she'd only snowboarded twice last season.

Rick checked his phone. "Gotta go."

"Me, too. Thanks for the company, ladies." Zander's eyes landed on Ivy, catching her staring. She quickly looked away.

"Any time. We're here every Tuesday." Penelope focused on Rick. Did he even notice her?

Zander followed Rick to the bar to settle his tab.

"No wonder you like Zander. He's dreamy." Sammy sipped her margarita.

"Dreamy? Who uses that word?" Ivy said, trying to make the conversation lighter.

"I like dreamy." Sammy pressed one palm against her cheek.

"I think he's swankolicious." Penelope fanned her face.

"And he seems interested in you, Ivy." Sammy got up and put her arm around her.

Deep down, she longed for a companion. That's why she had her cat, Marshmallow.

CHAPTER 13

Zander didn't make it to the skate park until Thursday afternoon. He hadn't been to a park since college and couldn't wait to try out some new tricks. Without his wings, he'd better not try a quadruple flip. A single time in Earth's heavier gravity would have to suffice.

Somebody did a burly aerial spin on the half-pipe ramp. A bold move. He held his breath until the skater landed. Then he spotted a woman on a pink board with pink skate shoes.

Ivy.

He waved to her.

With the board in hand, she walked over, her aura glowing an excited reddish-yellow. "Did you see my trick?"

"Sure did. You're incredibly talented."

"I felt like I was a bird."

"Look at your shoulders. You might be sprouting wings." If only this were true. If she lived in Cupid's Corner, he'd definitely date this cute athletic woman. Too bad she had to be human. The idea saddened him. He liked hanging out with her and her friends.

"Ever since I was a little kid, I've had dreams where I unfurled iridescent wings." She sighed. "I'd fly alongside brightly colored birds above a lush tropical rainforest."

"I've had similar dreams. Mine featured me soaring with dragonflies above a grassy meadow." He chuckled. "I can't believe I actually shared that."

"It is rather girlish."

"Don't you dare say that." He flexed his biceps. "I'm a hundred percent male."

She gave him an impish grin. Her phone rang, and she pulled it out of the front pocket of her backpack. "I need to get this." She walked to a bench at the side.

As long as she was busy, he'd try doing that flip. At the top of the half-pipe ramp, he took a deep breath. *I will do this.* With his right foot on the tail of the board, he stepped on the front, leaned forward, and sailed to the center. Bending his knees, he did a backside kick turn and shouted, "Yes!" Rotating his head to face the center, he rode low to the ground. Standing near the top, he did a double-flip. Getting air was almost like flying. Exhilaration zoomed through his blood as he kept the ride going. Completing at least a dozen passes, he landed on the top of the ramp, flipped the board into his hand, and walked toward the park's entrance.

"Not bad," Ivy said. "Next time, you should do a triple-flip."

"You weren't impressed."

She lifted a shoulder, but the corner of her mouth quirked.

"I thought we were friends, but now—"

She bumped him in the shoulder. "You were competent out there."

"That's not any better. Admit it. I look hot." He put his arm around her shoulder. "And since I'm off Sunday, you'll want to hang out with me."

"I've got to study for my tort class," she sighed. "It deals with civil injury lawsuits."

"Sounds complicated."

"It is."

"A couple of hours in a canoe will help clear your head. I'll do all the rowing."

She hesitated and stared at the ground. "Umm … I suppose I could swing two hours." She got on her board and zoomed off.

That's when he realized she'd been wearing dress slacks and a silky blouse, a total contrast to the pink sneakers and her backward cap.

IVY PARKED her Jeep in front of the Moosehead Campground and jogged to the rental shack. To the right of the dock, four or five jet skis were anchored. Dozens of kayaks, rowboats and canoes were tethered to the deck.

Zander waited for her in front of a canary yellow canoe. "Put on your life vest. The water's calling us.

"As long as we're back by noon." She buckled the front of her orange life vest.

He held up two fingers like a boy scout giving his promise. "You have my word."

She climbed in and sat on a bench in the back, putting her backpack on a board in the center.

He hopped in the seat in front facing her. "East or west?" he asked.

"West." Ivy stared at his ripped biceps as he picked up the oars. "Aren't you supposed to face the other way?"

"Where's the fun in that? I can't see you." He smiled. "And it'll be a lot harder to talk."

"You seem to have all the answers."

"Not at all." He put his oar in the water, pushing the blade away, taking the edge out of the water, and repeating the motion. They were gliding. His eyes twinkled.

They passed the campground filled with tents and travel trailers. " My cabin's just up that path. It's not much but beats living in a tent."

"Tents aren't bad. Bears can be a pain."

"Were you chased?" He asked, his deep tone serious.

"No. My mom forgot to hang our food bag in a tree, so in the middle of the night we heard a bear growling and ripping apart our campground near the fire pit. We banged pans inside the tent, and the bear eventually left." She laughed. "My mom and step-dad had been terrified, but I thought it was hilarious."

"Didn't you know bears have big claws and teeth?"

"Not at the time. Being little, I assumed the animals were fuzzy like my teddy bear."

"Does anything scare you?"

"Not really." That question threw her for a loop. She had learned to be tough at a young age. The only thing that truly frightened her at the moment was her building attraction to Zander. "Tell me about you're camping experiences."

"Never been. Staying in a cabin is the closest thing."

What a vague response. "Did you live in one place or move a few times?"

"One place. And you?"

Again, he redirected the conversation. Still, if she opened up, he might too. "We moved a lot. You're lucky you didn't."

"I never thought much about it."

"Did you live close to Lake Tahoe?"

"Not too far. We spent our summers swimming and boating." He shifted sideways to look at her. "There's a cove to our right. Let's head there."

"Works for me."

They maneuvered the canoe through a narrow entrance into a somewhat circular pool of water. Above them, brush and leafy trees filled the sloping hills. "It's hard to believe that lava formed this land. Weathering created this cove," she said as they pulled close to the shore.

"It's pretty." He set his paddle down and unzipped his backpack. "Want a power bar?"

"Sure." Sparks tingled from where their fingertips touched. She pulled out two water bottles and handed him one. In less than a minute, she had finished her snack and drink. The sun shone on her shoulders. "I'm going swimming." She peeled off her shorts and T-shirt down to her one-piece swimsuit and jumped over the side. The cool water revitalized her soul. She swam to a rock in the center of the cove and jumped onto the top to sit.

"You could have waited for me." Zander appeared in front of the rock and moved next to her.

She tried not to stare at his glistening, toned abs but couldn't help herself.

"You picked the ideal place to sun yourself."

"You make it sound like I'm a seal," she joked.

"A curvy and beautiful one." His eyes met hers, gazing at her as if she were a goddess. The intensity warmed her to her core as he leaned closer.

"Ahoy," someone shouted from the water. It turned out to be a kayaker.

"Hey," Zander answered. "Perfect day to be outside."

With the intense moment broken, she slipped into the water and swam to the canoe, hopped inside, and dried off with a towel from her backpack.

"I liked our swim." Water dripped off his body as he reached inside his backpack for a towel.

Damn, he was gorgeous. She checked the time on her phone. "It's quarter to eleven. Let's head back."

"You sure."

"I'm afraid so." She'd much rather stay right here and see if his kisses turned out to be as smoking as his body. She rarely took time for herself. He said she needed to unwind, and he had been absolutely right. "Thanks for inviting me today." He forced her to go outside and appreciate the pleasant summer day. Another few months and the air would turn chilly. She could have easily missed enjoying this summer in her lovely resort town.

"I get it. At home, I've been guilty of working too hard. But there's something special about this place."

"I agree. The moment I arrived here and took a deep breath, I connected with the positive vibes." She put on her shorts and T-shirt.

He paddled out of the cove and gave her a mischievous grin. "This town does grow on you."

Her heart did a silly loop. "I'm going river rafting with Sammy and her husband next Sunday. You wanna come?"

"Are you asking me on a date?" His brow lifted.

She shrugged. It might not be an answer, but that was all he'd be getting.

CHAPTER 14

At 10:04 a.m., a dually crew cab truck screeched to a halt in front of Zander's campground entrance to pick him up for the three-hour river rafting trip. Ginormous tires scattered dirt.

A window at the back rolled down. "Hop in on the other side."

He got in and buckled his seatbelt. The guy in the front turned his head and pushed up his Ray-Ban sunglasses. "Name's Darryl," he held out his hand.

Holy crap. Sammy's husband happened to be his release officer. Hopefully, he wouldn't remember. His stomach clenched as the truck pulled onto the highway.

"I can't wait to get out on the water." Ivy crossed her shapely legs and jiggled her foot.

He let out the breath he'd been holding.

"Me too. Ever been rafting?" Sammy asked.

"Not yet. Been boating and paddle boarding." Zander winked at Ivy.

"Love this song." Sammy turned up the radio. Country music twanged.

Ivy sang along. She could ride a skateboard like a pro, but her flat notes were a tinge off-key. In truth, he kinda liked that flaw. He'd never met anyone as intriguing as her. He'd been taught that Cupids were superior to humans in every way. After meeting Ivy, the logic seemed to fall short.

He nonchalantly glanced at her. Dark, luxurious locks were pulled back in a ponytail. Her chocolate-colored eyes were warm and inviting. Her full mouth tempted him, practically daring him for a kiss.

"Are you a native Idahoan?" he asked Sammy.

"Yep. Born and raised in Beaver Gulch about twenty miles south of Moosehead as the crow flies."

"The crow flies? You're funny." Cupids flew the most direct routes without thinking about it.

"How'd you and Darryl meet?"

"In college. We both went to Peregrine."

"Where's that?"

"In the panhandle about fifty miles south of Canada," Darryl said.

"In a psych class." She put her hand on her husband's shoulder.

"It took me three weeks to get the courage to ask her out. Figured she was out of my league. Still do."

"Enough about us. Zander, have you always lived in Heavenly Valley?" Sammy asked.

"Except for college, I've lived there my whole life." His future had been planned out since he was a cherub. Luckily, archery came easy, giving him plenty of time to play.

"Got you beat." Sammy clasped her hands together. "My folks live in a farmhouse built by my great-great-grandparents. They didn't even add plumbing until after my fifth birthday."

"My poor wife." Darryl reached for her hand.

Not interested in considering his own realm in Cupid's Corner`, he stared out the window. Would he ever make it back to Cupid's Corner or see his family? He missed his other life.

"You okay?" Ivy leaned closer.

"Just enjoying the view." He gazed into her dark eyes. "Beautiful."

"It is a pretty drive." The corners of her mouth lifted.

The truck curved along a windy road. "Our destination is right around the bend," Darryl said.

They entered Trout River city limits. He glanced at the fast-flowing river that ran beside the road on the left. It reminded him of the Fate River that bordered Cupid's Corner. They crossed a bridge, and the murky water ended up on their right. Two rafts bounced along some gnarly rapids. "That looks awesome."

"It is." Sammy and Ivy said in unison.

The truck screeched around a curve. Zander's hand landed against Ivy's smooth, toned thigh.

They turned off at a small building with Trout River Rafting painted on the side.

"We've got dibs on the front." Sammy high-fived her husband.

"Be my guest," Ivy whispered to Zander. "They'll be drenched when the rapids start."

"I like getting wet. Besides, I've got a waterproof camera. That way I won't drop my cell into the river like I did last time." Sammy scrunched up her face.

"You did that because you wanted a new phone." Darryl placed his arm around his wife.

The group walked inside the office, paid for their seats, signed waivers, were sized for life vests, and strapped themselves into fluorescent green ones.

"I look like a firefly." Zander joked.

Ivy rolled her eyes. She and Sammy headed toward the shore.

"Can I talk to you for a minute?" Darryl stepped next to Zander.

Uh-oh. This didn't sound good. "Sure. What's up?" Zander tried to keep his voice steady.

"Does Ivy know about your arrest?"

Shit. His palms got sweaty, and he rubbed them on his shorts. "No."

"Tell her."

"I will. Just not here. Later."

"Fine," he snapped. "Don't wait. I get that you made a mistake, but Ivy deserves the truth. These things have a way of showing up." Meaning he'd be talking with his wife. "Come on. The ladies are waiting. Just remember. I'll be watching you."

Zander walked next to Darryl and headed toward a couple standing near a neon orange raft where a pool of calm water led to the rapids.

A husky man walked up. "Welcome to the Trout River Rafting Excursion. I'm Bear, your guide. To ensure our safety, we'll go over a few rules. If you fall in, remember—on your back with your nose and toes to the sky."

Zanders eyes met Ivy's. She turned toward the guide who talked about the oars and how to paddle. "If there aren't any questions, let's get this trip started."

Ivy positioned herself in the middle on the left side. "I can't believe it's been a year since we came here."

"Me, neither," Sammy said.

Zander's hand brushed the side of her knee as he moved into the spot on her right. "This is cozy."

A slight smile graced her lips.

Sammy sat in front of Ivy. "I'm excited."

Darryl secured his spot in front of Zander. The guide hopped into the back and untied the rope. "Okay, folks. We're gonna have a rip-roaring time."

Zander held the T-grip at the top with his left hand and his right near the center. He dipped his blade in the water and paddled as the guide called out to stroke. The current pushed their raft along the river, calm and soothing at the moment as it meandered along. Several fishermen waded in a side tributary of the river, throwing out fish lines. Zander waved with his right hand. The men waved back.

"I could get into fishing here." Darryl patted his wife's hand.

"Not for me. Maybe you could talk Zander into going with you?"

"No thanks." He didn't believe in torturing fish with a hook.

Heat from the sun combined with the cool breeze coming off the water. The temperature perfect. The raft floated up and down with the flow of the river.

"You mentioned boating in Tahoe. Did you sail or use a speed boat?"

Once again, Ivy asked about his background. He tried to stick to the truth as much as possible. "My family owns a two-seater jet boat that practically flies through the water."

"Too bad you didn't bring it here. I'd like to give it a spin." Ivy's voice sounded dreamy.

It wasn't like he could invite her to Cupid's Corner and take her out on Lake Aphrodite, but a part of him wished he could.

"What about sailing? Have you ever done that?" Ivy asked.

"I've been a few times." He had to change topics and get away from his hometown.

"How 'bout you?"

"I once took a schooner to get to my grandmother's place.

She lives on an island near the Bahamas."

"What island?" He had been to the Bahamas once in the last year and found the setting peaceful.

"Rhapsody."

"I like the name." Why did it ring a bell? He hadn't been there before but recalled some significance with the place.

"Rapids ahead," Bear called.

A leap of water came crashing toward the raft, sloshing everyone inside.

"I needed that," he nudged Ivy.

She gave a faraway look. "It amazes me how it took thousands of years for the water to cut through those rocks and form this canyon."

"It is a phenomenal place."

"You've got that right." Sammy's head bobbed with the water.

The raft floated downstream, the rhythm of the waves moving them through rough patches. Rapids swirled underneath, they hit a bump, and Ivy gripped his knee.

"Latch onto me whenever you'd like."

"Aw, how sweet," Sammy sighed.

"Why thank you," he said with a smile.

"Wipe that grin off and keep paddling," Ivy snorted. "We're heading for some boulders."

"Sure thing." He saluted her.

Ahead, he spotted a tight passage where the river narrowed between several boulders. The group maneuvered through it with the help of their oars.

"Rapids ahead. High side. Right paddle back," Bear shouted. "Brace the oars. Square off."

The raft bounced off a rock and spun around. Light shone near his feet, and he looked for the source. Something from Ivy's ankle illuminated white. She must be wearing an ankle bracelet. They went up and slammed down.

"Watch out," Ivy shouted.

A wave hit the side and caught the boat in the crest. The momentum threw Zander. He toppled into the murky river and plunged underwater. There was no sense of up and down. He held his breath. Starved for oxygen. Trying to get his bearings. What did Bear say to do? Somehow, he reached the surface, his hand latched onto an oar, and someone pulled him back inside the boat.

"You're wet." Ivy eyed his soggy shirt that fit him like a skin and blushed.

Floating inside a rubber raft in wet clothes, Zander couldn't stop grinning as their trip continued.

"We're almost to the Salmon Campground where the trip ends," Bear interrupted with a booming voice. "You can get something to eat at the snack bar."

"Works for me. I'm starving. When we get to the outskirts of Moosehead, we'll eat dinner at the Cattleman's Club," Daryl said. "They've got fantastic barbecued ribs."

"We're at this gorgeous setting, and all you can think about is your stomach." Sammy laughed as the raft floated along the river.

"Men," Ivy added with a chuckle.

CHAPTER 15

The truck approached the Moosehead Campground around seven.

"I've got a bottle of wine and thought about watching the sunset on the shore. Anyone else interested in joining me?" Zander asked.

"Sure." Ivy wasn't ready for her day to end. She liked spending time with Zander.

Darryl's scowl said he didn't like the idea. "Not for me. Got an early shift tomorrow."

Ivy would be alone with Zander—as friends of course. Resisting her wicked attraction had tormented her all day. It might take every ounce of her control to keep her desire for him at bay.

The truck pulled off into the dirt in front of the state

park, and everyone said their goodbyes. He and Ivy walked through the double gates.

"I've never been inside this campground. It's nice."

"The setting's not bad, however my cabin is pretty primitive."

"Your version of camping, right?" She recalled a previous conversation.

"Exactly," Zander said as they veered at the third pathway on the right. His mussed hair gave him a sexy, just out of bed look.

She stepped inside a room about the size of her closet, glanced around his cabin, expecting to see clothes strewn across the floor like most bachelors' rooms. The bed was made. The place tidy.

"What do you think of my humble abode?" He gave her a lop-sided smirk, and her heart beat faster.

"It's cozy."

"That's a polite way to describe it. At least I went shopping yesterday." He lifted the lid of an ice chest. "We could have grapes, cheese, and cherry tomatoes with our wine."

"Sounds good." There seemed to be an awkwardness between them that she couldn't quite figure out.

He put the food in Ziplock baggies, grabbed a vinyl lunch bag off his dresser, and handed it to her. He held up a bottle of Chardonnay. "Not sure how good Moosehead Vineyards will be."

"It's not bad."

He carried the wine and placed a towel over his shoulder, and they were walking again.

"Hey Zander." A young couple with a baby waved from across the way.

He smiled, waved back but didn't converse. People along the shoreline gathered their things to go home. "I like to jog early in the morning when most folks are still sleeping." He kept their pace leisurely.

Her breath caught as she stared at the glassy turquoise water. "This is stunning."

"We can sit here." He spread out his towel. His blue eyes sparkled when he gazed at her, and her insides quivered.

Sunlight flickered off the lake as water lapped along the shore. "It's peaceful."

A bullfrog croaked.

"Is he trying to scare us off?" She unzipped the lunch bag.

"Probably just singing for his lady." He got out a wine opener from his pocket and struggled with the bottle, but managed to get out the cork, poured it into paper cups, and handed one to her. "Hope this is fancy enough for you?"

"It's great." She took a sip.

"I'm glad you came." He drank his wine.

"Me, too." The odd tension between them bothered her. Their easy friendship apparently had changed. "Tell me your deepest, darkest fear?" She finished her wine and poured more into her cup and his.

He stared at her.

"You have to be afraid of something?" She had to get him

to open up.

He paused for a few seconds. "If you must know, I'm claustrophobic. Can't stand to be closed in."

"Any reason why?"

"I must've been about four or five and played hide-and-seek with my older brothers. Thought I'd been pretty clever when I snuck into the attic, opened up a chest full of clothes, and slipped inside. Then the lid slammed down. I was trapped. It may have only been minutes, but it felt like hours."

"You must've been terrified." She pictured him as an adorable little towhead.

"To say the least. Even now I avoid closed-in spaces including elevators."

"In my building, I prefer taking the stairs, but I do that to get in extra steps."

He eyed her calves. "It shows."

Her cheeks grew warm.

"Wanna tell me what made you get that rose tattoo on your ankle?"

"It's not a tattoo—it's a birthmark." She'd inherited the weird mark from her father's side of the family.

"Gives us something in common." He held up the heart on his wrist. "Mine comes with special powers."

"I suppose you cast spells on unsuspecting women," she couldn't resist taunting.

"Did it work?"

"Not one iota." She lied. The more she got to know

Zander, the more she liked him.

"Were you wearing an ankle bracelet earlier?"

"No." That question was off the wall.

"When we were on the raft, I could've sworn I saw light sparkling from your ankle. It distracted me, and that's why I fell overboard." His mouth quirked upward.

"Good excuse."

"It's the truth. Now your turn. What scares you?" His gaze became intense.

"Spiders."

"You've just ruined your tough gal persona."

"I'm not tough, just determined." Life had taught her plenty.

He refilled their cups with the rest of the bottle and stuffed the empty container in his backpack. "The sun's dipping down."

The sky turned to a pinkish-orange, and she got up and walked to the water's edge. A hint of pink tinted the dark blue horizon. He stood next to her, his arm slipped around her shoulders. She leaned into him, mindful of his brawny arms and well aware of how good his body looked in swim trunks.

He threaded his fingers through her hair, gazing at her with a hunger that made her breathless, filling her with a promise that might take their friendship in another direction.

"Soft and silky. Figured it'd be that way." His mouth came close. As she anticipated their lips meeting, he pressed against hers, causing an electric thrill where they met. Then he pulled away and cocked his head as his eyes darkened with desire. "Couldn't resist you." The briefest brush of his lips, and she'd swear their contact sizzled. Her lips continued tingling. The sun dropped in the sky reminding her of a scene in a romantic movie.

ZANDER KISSED a mortal not once but twice. Forbidden. Wrong. Delightful.

A buzz charged through his veins. He'd never felt so connected after a simple kiss. Simple? Not with the flames that sparked between them.

"Thanks for sharing the sunset with me." Her voice came out soft and sexy. Using her phone as a flashlight, she helped him pack up their things.

"It was my pleasure." He held her hand as they walked along the path, appreciating her company. This would be a good time to tell her about the arrest.

Not yet, he told himself.

Next time.

They waited for a car to pass, crossed the street, and sat at the trolley stop bench. She flipped her hair behind her shoulder and gave him a slow, sensual smile.

He leaned down and sampled her lips. They were softer and more tempting than any female he'd ever kissed. She stirred his imagination with wild fantasies.

CHAPTER 16

Friday around five, Ivy carried her skateboard and took the stairs down to the lobby. All week, Ivy kept reliving that kiss they'd shared last Sunday. She liked Zander, but he'd be leaving soon.

Zander stood there holding a single white rose.

"Weren't we meeting at the restaurant?" Ivy asked, surprised to see him.

He gave her a roguish grin. "I'm done for the day and figured we could go together."

He held the door for her as she walked out. The moment they set their boards on the sidewalk, they soared along Hemlock Avenue. Two and a half blocks into their ride, crowds filled the walkway on Lakeshore Drive, forcing both of them to pick up their boards and carry them.

"Do these crowds bother you?"

"Not really. It's only crazy for a few months in the summer and most vacationers are nice. Winter gets busy, but nothing like this."

They reached the shoreline. Someone parasailed by. "Have you ever tried that?"

"Something about parachutes scares me." She tried not to shudder.

"Coming from a woman who can land a triple flip on a half-pipe. You do have an Achille's heel, so to speak," he said chuckling.

"Like you won't step inside an elevator?"

"Touché." He held the Lakeshore Pizza door for her.

"I'm starving." She glanced around the room. "It's packed. Let's get a table in the bar."

They found one in the corner and ordered a carafe of white wine to go with their half veggie, half pepperoni pizza.

"How's your week been?" he set his arm on the back of her seat.

"Swamped with work." Which was true.

"Any plans for the weekend?"

"Layout by the pool and catch up on some reading. Other than that, nothing."

"I'm off Sunday and thought about checking out Moosehead's archery range. Wanna join me?" His blue eyes twinkled as he regarded her. "It'd be a lot more enjoyable with a friend."

Ivy liked hanging out with him. She liked Zander and

wouldn't mind another date with him. "I'll go. Just so you know, I've never tried archery."

"I'm an expert marksman. If you need any help, let me know."

"That's right. Your family owns a bow and arrow company."

He shrugged. Strange. He had no trouble saying he was an expert but almost seemed embarrassed his family owned a factory.

A waitress delivered their pizza. Ivy had skipped lunch and finished her first slice in what seemed like seconds.

"Did it take much schooling to become a paralegal?"

"I got my certificate while I was working on my bachelor's."

"Where'd you go to college?" He reached for the last slice of pizza. "You mind?"

"Go ahead." She'd had her fill, but it still surprised her he asked.

He picked off the pepperoni and ate the piece. "You were telling me about college?"

"I went to Boise State."

"How far is that from here?"

"About three hours. What I liked about living in the state capital was I had access to the Idaho State Law Library." She learned to love the musky smell of the room.

"What made you come here?"

"A change of pace." She was not about to bring up her idiot ex. "Where did you go to college?"

"A small campus in Lover's Landing. I majored in … business."

She wondered why he hesitated but didn't call him on it. "Where's Lover's Landing?"

"… Nevada. Not far from Tahoe."

A yawn escaped, and she covered her mouth. "I'm more tired than I realized."

"Another late night studying."

"Finishing a paper that was due today. Thanks for dinner."

He paid the bill. "I'll walk you home."

"It's out of your way."

"I don't mind. Is there a trolley stop near you?" He gave her an endearing grin.

"On Lynx Street." She stared at his mouth and recalled the kisses they shared. The thought of his firm lips against hers made her insides quiver.

He held the door for her and took her hand as they strolled along Lakeshore Drive, neither of them in a hurry. Light shimmered flickering gold over the lake. A breeze made the walk perfect.

"This is nice." His deep baritone voice warmed her heart.

"Summer's my favorite season." Zander seemed to make her take time to appreciate her world. "What about you?"

"Winter with snowcapped mountains and powdery snowboarding trails. Although summer here does have its advantages." His eyes held a mischievous glint.

"You're such a flirt."

They continued up the street. With few people out, she pulled her skateboard from her backpack and said, "Race you to the corner of Red Cedar." She took off on her board.

"That's not fair," he shouted.

Not about to impede her momentum, she didn't look back. Slowing only when she reached Cardinal Way and had to stop for a service van.

He rolled up next to her and chuckled. "You always so quick?"

"Only when I aim to win." They glided along the sidewalk side by side. The business district dropped to residential homes, and she breathed in the fresh scent. "I've been cooped up all day. I needed to get out tonight."

"Since I've never been to your place, do we turn on Red Cedar?"

"It's to the right, then take the second walkway on the left."

When they got to the sidewalk, she said, "I carry my board through here just in case there's a person walking around the bend."

"Did you ever run into someone?" He kicked his board into his hand.

"No, but I came close to taking out a fluffy little poodle."

"With all the bushes, this place looks more like a park than condos." He draped his arm around her shoulder.

She leaned closer. "That's one thing that hooked me on this place. The second was most people use these condos for vacation homes or rentals. They're rarely occupied."

"You're not only beautiful but smart."

She tried to stifle a sigh, but one slipped out anyway. "Does that line work on others?"

"Don't know. I've never tried it before."

"Yeah, right?" She stepped out of his arms and pulled out her key. "I'm in 3C."

"I like the red door. Does it bring you good fortune?"

"Once in a while." Like right now.

He brought his mouth close, his warm lips pressed against hers, and tingles spread through her body as he deepened the kiss. Then he pulled away and cocked his head to gaze at her with those eyes that were bluer than the lake. "Meet me at the archery range around ten."

"I'll be there." The handsome man reeled her in.

CHAPTER 17

Zander arrived early and rented equipment for the two of them. The place reminded him of home. Would anyone ever find him?

Eventually.

He'd survived several weeks already, and it had been okay. Working at a skate shop had not only been easy, but the job gave him extra money.

He glanced around the range. Bales of hay stacked four high and strategically spread out near the back fence. A couple dozen paper targets had been tacked to the front of the hay. Normally, he used stand-up targets or virtual models but figured firing into the straw would be easy.

"Hi." Ivy walked up in short shorts that showed off her tanned legs. Her T-shirt saying, *Classy and Sassy,* described her personality.

"I take it the gray and pink bow's mine." She motioned to the ground. "But if I'm wrong, black's okay."

"Smart ass." He handed her the bow and a quiver with pink and purple feathered fletchings near the arrows' nock. "We're on targets five and six. You've never done this before?" Cupids had bows put in their hands as soon as they could walk.

"But I have shot a gun and even drove a race car on a drag strip."

"Impressive. Who's car?" He'd raced his chariot before but never on a racetrack.

"My brother, Jed, tried racing for a while. Without a sponsor, it got too expensive."

This stint on Earth had shown him how money could make or break you. It was much easier creating whatever you needed with magic. "How many brothers and sisters do you have?"

"One brother, two sisters."

She mentioned they all had different fathers. Having one father his whole life, he wondered what it had been like for her. "You're the oldest, right?"

"I am. Jed is three years younger. He's a mechanic in Boise."

"Are you close?"

"Of all my siblings, I relate the best with him." She sighed. "We're both so busy I hardly ever see him. What about your siblings?"

"I'm the youngest of three boys."

"Thus, you grew up spoiled."

"Not at all. My older brothers were pretty good at putting me in my place." He'd rather not talk about how ruthlessly competitive his brothers were. "You ready for some pointers on shooting?"

"Sure, but later on, I'd like to hear more about your family."

They stopped behind the line for the target where about a dozen people in varying ages shot. "Do I use a skateboard stance?"

"Pretty close, but you stay on the balls of your feet. Hold the bow by the grip and let it fall into the pocket of your hand."

"Like this." She grasped her bow stiffly.

"That's it. Relax your fingers." He'd been dying to touch her and placed his arms around her shoulders. "Nock the end of the arrow in the middle of the string. Draw and anchor the bow like this. The elbow on your release arm should point straight away from the target with the forearm parallel to the ground." He helped her pull back. "Aim for the center. Release."

The arrow sailed straight into the bullseye.

"You're amazing." She gave him a beaming grin.

He'd taken his skill for granted. Cupids idolized him for his talent but seeing awe in Ivy's gaze pulled at his heart. He stepped back and lost the wonderful buzz of warmth from Ivy's closeness. "Try it on your own."

He watched her lips press together. Her posture stiffened

as she pulled back the string. She aimed. The arrow hit the outer white ring.

"By the end of this session, I bet you'll be showing me up."

"Not if you keep staring at me. Go on. Have your own fun." She shooed him to stand in front of his target a couple of feet from hers.

He picked up his bow. It had been over a month since he last shot. The rented bow was a trifle heavier than his own. Nevertheless, it felt like an old friend. Several seconds later, he sailed six arrows into his target and glanced in Ivy's direction.

Her eyes lit with appreciation. "You said you were good, but you're world-class."

"Thanks."

She shot, and the arrow landed in the grass. "You distracted me."

"Did I?" He couldn't resist kissing her cheek.

"How about some pointers?" she asked.

"Keep your eye on the arrow all the way to the target, and you'll have it."

She followed his guidance. Her arrow sailed into the second red ring. Her arms around his neck, and she hugged him. "I did it, Zander!"

A guy called into a megaphone, "Bows down." The announcer waited until everyone had stopped shooting. "Safety always comes first. I will count to ten. When I say retrieve, you may collect your arrows."

That took a couple of minutes.

For the next round, Zander zipped his arrows into the target in a straight line starting with the black circle. He even slowed his last arrow with a spiral twirl.

"Hey Zander." A familiar-looking man held out his hand. "Name's Brutus. You helped me carry boxes into the food bank."

"Oh—right—hi." Zander recalled meeting him on one of his first days in town.

"Where'd you learn to shoot like that?" Brutus asked.

"His family manufactures bows and arrows," Ivy called. "And he'd better teach me that last trick."

"When you're ready." He set down his bow and sidled closer to her spot. "Once you've mastered shooting."

Brutus moved on and chatted with other customers. Good because Zander would rather look at Ivy.

"I'm trying." She closed her eyes for a moment. "The arrow refuses to listen."

"Unless you take charge, they tend to have a mind of their own," he joked. "Show me how you aim, and I might be able to figure out what's wrong."

She pulled and released.

"Don't use your arms. Use your back muscles by squeezing your shoulder blades together as you pull back." He placed his arms over hers. "Imagine you're hitting the center when you release and watch it sail in place."

She tried again. "I did it! I made it in the yellow circle." She set down her bow and hugged him. "Thanks for the tip."

"Any time?" Especially if it ended with her body pressed against his.

Their session concluded, and they went inside to return the equipment.

Ivy grabbed a paper from the counter. "You should enter that contest."

He read the flyer. A tournament on July Fourth. The winning prize—$1000. The entry fee—fifty dollars. "Where do I sign up for this?" he asked the clerk.

"I can do it for you."

Zander handed the man his license and credit card. Then he said to Ivy, "Are you going to sign up?"

"Give me a year, and I'll smoke you." Her chin lifted, and she winked at him.

"Not likely." Knowing Ivy, she'd be a pro before summer was over.

CHAPTER 18

Moosehead Courthouse, July 2nd

Zander fiddled with his tie as he waited outside the courthouse. He hated the idea that his fate lay in the hands of an unknown human judge. Thank Zeus the state prosecution dismissed his public intoxication charge two weeks ago. Still, disturbing the peace could have a fine of up to a thousand dollars and or six months in jail. Given his clean record, he hoped to get the whole case dropped.

If only he could cross his wings for good measure. With wings, he could fly to Cupid's Corner instead of facing this judgment—but he wasn't ready to leave Ivy yet. He glanced at the clock on the wall. 9:33. Tugging at his pinstriped jacket, the borrowed suit fit a little loose.

His lawyer's shoes clicked on the linoleum as he walked

up wearing an Armani suit. Jim Brown shook Zander's hand. "Ready?"

"Let's get this over with." Zander stood next to his lawyer in the courtroom. Similar to the Cupid's Council chamber where his uncle worked, the additional platform under the judge's oak table made his position higher than the other furnishings. Except, this wasn't a friendly visit.

"Your Honor, I am asking that you suspend Mr. Eros sentence. He had a clean record before his arrest. While awaiting his arraignment, the defendant found employment at the Caribou Board Shop." Jim Brown said in a straightforward tone.

A woman typed on some sort of device near the judge's bench.

"If the defendant pays a $250 fine, I'm willing to drop the charges—after a period of six months providing there are no more infractions of the law within that time frame. Mr. Alexander Eros, do you accept the terms I've outlined for disturbing the peace?"

He looked at his lawyer. "Should I take this?"

"Yes." His lawyer nodded. "It's more than fair."

Zander agreed. He stood and said to the judge. "I do, Your Honor." He let out the breath he'd been holding.

"Mr. Brown's office will receive notice from the court about your final hearing date by the end of the week. Pay the cashier on the way out," the judge said.

He followed the lawyer through the center of the galley and past seven people waiting in other seats.

"This was nerve-wracking," Zander said. "How can you stand going to court?"

"Actually, I like it. Every case is unique." He slowed near the cashier. "Stop by my office later this afternoon, and we'll settle your bill."

"I will. Thanks again for your council."

"You're welcome." His lawyer walked off.

After waiting for three people in line, Zander paid his fine. He turned toward the exit and practically ran into Ivy. Oh no! His pulse shot through his veins.

"What are you doing here?" From her hair up in a tight bun to her skirt that landed just below her knees, Ivy appeared all business. She removed her hot pink spectacles. The way she eyed his suit said she wondered what was up.

Okay. Either he could try to make up a lie about being at the courthouse or tell the truth.

"Let me guess. You're paying off a parking ticket?" She canted her head and smiled.

"Not exactly." He could feel his cheeks heat. Darn it. "We need to talk. Do you have time to grab lunch?" No doubt after today, things between them would change. Why didn't he tell her the truth the day they went river rafting?

"I'm done here and have the next hour free." Her tone came out stifled and flat.

They walked outside and sat at a bench near the corner of Pepper Wood Way. She took off her high heels, grabbed a pair of sneakers from her briefcase, and laced them. "What? My feet hurt."

"I'm impressed you could even stand on those stilts at all." He wanted to say that her legs looked sexier in heels.

"Years of practice." She set her skateboard on the ground. "Where's your board?"

"I didn't bring it."

"Zander, what's going on?"

"Well." Admitting he was less than perfect wasn't easy.

"You can tell me." Compassion filled her dark eyes.

"I had a court hearing today." He walked next to her as she skated.

"You were arrested?"

He sucked in a deep breath. "You know my ex got married on the day before I arrived in town."

She nodded.

"Umm … I played blackjack at the Moosehead Saloon that night and ended up getting smashed." He shrugged. "I know. It was really stupid."

She moved slowly next to him.

"Then this guy came into the bar with a woman that looked like my ex. When I went up to him and cocked my fist, the alcohol did the thinking." He shook his head. "Not a smart move."

"Doesn't sound good."

"It gets worse. Some guy slapped cuffs on me, threw me in the back of a squad car, and I spent the night in jail."

"Jail? I bet that was rough." Her lips pressed together.

"It was. I never want to do that again."

"What happened with your case?"

"The charges will get dropped after six months' probation."

"It could be worse."

He couldn't read her expression.

They stopped outside Best Burgers. "Did Darryl arrest you?"

"Nope. He released me the next morning."

"Now I get why he acted funny when we went rafting." They headed for the counter.

"Are we still okay?" He had to know.

"I think so. I just wish you would have told me the truth earlier."

"So do I." He let out a long breath.

"No more secrets, okay?" She put one hand on her hip. "I hate liars."

"You've got it." He'd be honest with her about everything—except his Cupid life. That one he'd keep to himself.

"Good." She stepped up to the clerk at the counter. "Bacon King Burger, extra cheese, curly fries, and a large Coke." She turned to Zander. "What do you want?"

"Avocado veggie burger, sweet potato fries, iced tea."

"Veggie when you can have the real deal. You're nuts." She narrowed her eyes at him, paid with her debit card, and handed him a cup. They filled their drinks at the fountain and took a booth with a window view.

"Are you heading back to Heavenly after the Fourth of July?"

Like he had any idea if or when he'd get back to Cupid's

Corner. Still, this town had started to grow on him, as had spending time with Ivy. "I'll probably stick around until the skateboard shop slows, but at some point I'll have to go back."

Her brow lifted. "What does your family say about your extended vacation?"

"I've been a part of the business all my life. As the youngest son not much has been expected of me." He knew nothing about manufacturing arrows, and it bugged him to have to fabricate a story.

"And you came here to get away from your ex."

"Now that I've been away from Cami, I realize we didn't belong together. I dodged an arrow, so to speak."

A dreamy smile curved the corners of her mouth. "You mean a bullet?"

"That works, too."

The clerk brought out their food. Ivy dipped a fry in ketchup.

"You're coming to the archery contest Saturday, right?"

"Several of us already have tickets. If you win, we'll go out and celebrate." She sipped her drink. That sassy smile of hers drew him in.

He leaned over and brushed his lips against hers. "Don't you worry. I'll win."

CHAPTER 19

July Fourth

The Moosehead Archery Range bleachers were filling up fast with adults and teens, couples, and families with children. It was almost three, and the event would star soon, but the only one Ivy wanted to see was Zander.

"You've watched him shoot. Is he really that good?" Sammy rubbed her hands together.

"Definitely." A thrill shot through Ivy's veins and not because of his impressive marksmanship. She recalled him cocooning her in his arms when he instructed her on her aim.

Sammy put her hand above her eyes and squinted. "There's Penelope."

Ivy picked up her binoculars and zeroed in on Zander,

waiting behind the line while wearing a grin that created those adorable dimples. Confident. Dashing. Charismatic.

"You were checking Zander out. Let me see those." Sammy nabbed the field glasses.

Ivy pulled out her phone and scrolled her messages.

"This should be entertaining." Penelope plunked on the bench next to her. "Does it bug you Zander got arrested?"

"Maybe a little."

"I'd be miffed. I mean, if you hadn't run into him at the courthouse, you'd never know." Sammy sipped her soda.

"We all make mistakes. Besides, we're just friends, skating buddies."

"I'm not buying that. You like him." Penelope gave her a sideways glance.

Hell, yes, she did. He'd managed to worm his way into her life which scared the crap out of her.

Zander turned to the stands and waved.

"Any idea how much longer he'll be in town?" she asked Penelope.

"He hasn't mentioned taking him off the schedule yet." Penelope pulled out a bottle of water from her purse. "If he wins today, he said he might stick around a little longer. He's a great employee, on time, good with the customers even if he is a bit cocky."

"That's Zander." Ivy preferred to think about the sweet guy who had watched the sunset with her.

"There's nothing wrong with having a little fun as long as you remember he's a vacationer. They always leave." Still suffering from her last breakup, Penelope gave her a half-hearted grin.

"I know." Just like most of the men in Ivy's life. A pain shot straight through her heart. "Don't make a big deal out of it. We've only been on a couple of dates."

"But you're falling for him." Sammy gave her the I-know-you-too-well look.

As if sensing her thoughts, he turned to the stands and waved. Even knowing he was addressing the crowd, her breath stopped and a delirious giddiness filled her from deep within her soul.

"Welcome, ladies and gentlemen," the announcer's voice came out through the speakers.

The archers were introduced. Each stood several yards away from one of the eight targets spread out along the field. Zander took his position behind the fifth target holding his rented precision bow and quiver with arrows.

"Folks, there will be five rounds of shooting," the announcer said. "The competition begins with each archer taking his turn, one shot at a time from eighty yards. Once three arrows are shot, points will be tallied. Then the archers remove their arrows. This process continues four more times. Two at ninety and two at a hundred yards. When that is completed, the points are totaled. The best score wins the money."

"Easy enough to follow." Sammy smiled.

"We'll begin with some practice shots." The announcer

blew a whistle, and arrows sailed into the targets. Zander finished before the others, all three inside the center ring.

Ivy kept her eyes on Zander. He didn't seem the least bit edgy. Come to think of it, the only time Zander ever seemed a bit jittery was when she had approached him at the courthouse. Moving around as much as she had as a kid, Ivy faked self-assurance until one day she believed in herself, while Zander appeared to come about poise naturally.

Round one began, and the first contestant shot. Ivy looked through her binoculars. His arrow landed in the gold ring. The second and third archers had direct hits. The fourth stuck on the line between the yellow and red.

Then Zander got his turn. Her stomach twisted as he pulled back on the string and released the arrow.

"Go, Zander," Penelope shouted.

Dead center.

Ivy clapped, as did her friends.

"Let me see those binoculars?" Sammy asked.

"Sure." Ivy handed them to her.

The three of them took turns using Ivy's field glasses as the tournament went on. The next two contenders hit their marks, while the last one hit outside the black ring. Zander didn't hesitate during his next turn—just sailed his arrow into the bullseye.

"He makes it look easy." Ivy sighed.

"Where'd he learn to shoot like that?" Sammy asked.

"Supposedly, he had a bow in his hand the moment he

could walk." Ivy could almost picture him. With those gorgeous blue eyes, he must've been a charmer.

"Some parents are like that. Tiger Woods held his first club when he was two," Penelope said.

"Who?" Both Ivy and Sammy said in unison.

"He's an old guy my grandma keeps hoping will make a comeback."

"Relatives can be so weird. My grandfather has a wall filled with Dale Earnhardt memorabilia, and the guy died in 2001." Sammy scratched her head.

"And you'll inherit everything one day." Ivy laughed.

"Gramps promised the things to my brother which is fine with me."

"After our first round, Eros and Jones tied for first with thirty points, Smith and Williams tied for second with 29, and third place is Gonzales with 28," the announcer called. "It's still anyone's game at this point." The contestants move back to the second line.

"Jones is pretty good. He was the first alternate at the last Olympics." Sammy fanned her face.

"Zander should be on the Olympic team." The words came out on their own accord.

"Did he ever try out? I'm curious." Sammy put her hand on Ivy's shoulder.

"I have no idea."

After the third round, Zander had a one-point lead. Ivy couldn't help smiling.

"Our last two rounds move to one hundred yards away," the announcer said.

"He's gonna win this." Sammy clenched her fists.

When one of the contestants missed his shot at the first target, a resounding "awe" came from the audience.

"What happened?" Penelope asked.

"The guy's arrow sailed over the top." Ivy handed her friend the binoculars.

Zander had finesse. Ivy chewed her bottom lip as his final arrow spiraled into the gold center next to the other two. "Yes!" she got up, adjusting her binoculars to focus on him.

He waved to the audience. His smile seemed practiced. Nothing like the smile he gave her when he'd just mastered a skateboarding trick or when he'd paddle boarded next to her on the lake.

Sammy stood and bounced on her toes. "Zander's a superstar."

"Tied for third with one-hundred-forty-six points, Jesse Gonzales and Nick Roberts. Second place with one-hundred-forty-eight points, Mel Jones," the announcer called. "Our winner with a perfect score and some fancy shooting—Zander Eros."

A rip-roaring standing ovation followed.

Handed a gigantic check for $1,000, Zander did a victory dance.

"What a ham!" Penelope gave a goofy grin.

"Let's go down there and congratulate him," Sammy said

while already stepping into the aisle. Once they reached the grass, she asked, "Who's that talking with him?"

"Brutus Johansen, the owner of this archery range." Zander had introduced her to him when they came here on a date.

Others crowded around Zander, patting him on the back, congratulating him. He spotted her and walked in her direction. "Told you I'd win."

"And you never brag," Ivy teased.

"Zander, you were awesome." Penelope high-fived him. "We're heading for Lynx. Wanna join us?"

His eyes caught with Ivy's as if asking for permission.

She nodded.

"I'd love to, but I could use a ride."

"After that stellar performance, anything for you, Zander. Then let's get going. I'm ready to celebrate. I'm pretty sure Ivy said she's buying the first round." Penelope laughed.

CHAPTER 20

Zander smiled at Ivy who sat to his right with his arm around the back of her chair. A triumph usually brought him euphoria, and he was happy he won but mostly because of the admiring gleam in Ivy's eyes as she gazed at him.

He liked this mortal. An inkling of guilt flittered through his conscience, but he pushed the notion away. Today was for celebration.

"In honor of Zander's victory. Give us a round of Kamikaze shooters—on my tab." Ivy brushed her hand along his leg.

The waitress squinted at Zander. "What are you celebrating?"

"He won the archery tournament. You should have seen

him nail every shot." Sammy's gushing exuberance was sweet.

"Congrats. You must be exceptional," the waitress said.

"I try." The dynamics between him and Ivy had changed in a good way. He couldn't resist taking her hand in his.

"Wish I could have been there to see it." Rick moved into the empty spot by Penelope.

"Is there anything else I can get you?"

"Mozzarella sticks and onion rings on me," Penelope said, and the waitress left.

Got any plans for that thousand dollars you won?" Sammy asked.

"I'm thinking about sticking around for a little longer." He pulled out a card from his pocket. "Brutus just offered me a position at the range to run the junior archery club and several tournaments."

Ivy canted her head. "You considering it?"

"Maybe for a month or two, but we haven't talked money yet." Since he had no idea when or if he'd ever leave Moosehead, the job sounded like a good plan.

"No hasty decisions. I still need you to open tomorrow." Penelope pointed at him.

"Yes, boss." He saluted her.

The waitress dropped off their drinks.

Penelope toasted, "To Zander."

They clicked glasses.

"My roommate's moving out in two weeks. If you're

sticking around for a couple of months, you should rent his room? Four-fifty a month. Split utilities," Rick said.

"Let me think about it." Zander had just got used to cabin living, plus Rick was a friend and he didn't like leaving him in the lurch if an opportunity to go back to Cupid's Corner arrived. "I'll let you know next week."

Appetizers were passed around.

"Now for the million-dollar question. Why aren't you on the U.S. Olympic team?" Sammy leaned an elbow on the table.

"Never tried out." Not on Earth. No need as an elite Cupid archer.

"You should dude." Rick crunched on an onion ring.

The table ordered dinner. Ivy's head dipped while she nonchalantly glanced at him. Enticing and gorgeous. He'd like to get her away from here and kiss her senseless.

Dinner was delivered. He bit into his veggie burger.

A DJ played "Love Someone."

"You know what that means," Penelope called.

"Everyone dances," Sammy said.

A favorite in Cupid's Corner, Zander knew this line dance. He offered his hand to Ivy, and she took it. Tingles arced from the simple touch. This strong connection had to mean something. What? He wasn't sure.

On the dance floor, his attention drifted toward Ivy as she swiveled and mambo stepped in her pink shorts and her favorite Etnies skater shoes. The ones he had sold her when she first visited Caribou's.

Ivy bumped into him. "Sorry." She gave him a slight grin.

"I'm not."

The song ended, forcing everyone back to their table for another round of drinks.

Rick's phone chirped. "I'm joining some friends to watch fireworks down at the marina. Anyone else wanna join me?"

"I'm in." Penelope pushed a strand of her brown hair behind her ear.

"Not tonight. Darryl's picking me up soon."

"I'll pass. It gets pretty hectic down there." Ivy put her hand on his knee, the warmth of her fingers charging fire deep in his belly. She whispered to him, "I'd rather watch them from my balcony. You interested?"

Maybe it was the alcohol or the hours spent in the sun, but whatever brought about this idea made his heart soar.

"You guys have fun." Zander's words came out choked, and he downed his Long Island Iced Tea, his heart drumming in his ears because Ivy had invited him to her place. "This sure has a kick." Zander draped his arm around Ivy's shoulders. She leaned against him.

Boots clicked on the floor. Darryl walked toward them. "Hey." Dressed in his police uniform, Darryl sat by his wife and turned to Zander. "Sorry I missed your tournament. Heard you were awesome out there today."

"Thanks."

"I've never seen anything like him. He didn't just shoot; he added a spin and the arrow spiraled into the bullseye." Sammy spoke fast. "You should have heard the crowd cheer."

"Congratulations, Zander. Ready to go home?" Darryl asked Sammy.

"You bet." The couple walked out.

"It's the two of us. Wanna dance or … go back to my place?" Ivy said slow and sultry.

Would they make out while watching the fireworks?

"Well?" Her eyes flickered.

Unable to resist her offer, he said, "Your place?" He'd finally get to have her to himself alone and see what developed.

CHAPTER 21

Along with being slightly tipsy, Ivy's emotions were a combination of giddiness and fear. A part of her said she was crazy inviting Zander to her place, but after a year-long dry spell . . . she wanted him.

Holding hands, they strolled up Lynx Street and crossed at Blue Burch.

"I had a good time tonight," he said.

"So did I." They walked another block, crossed Red Cedar Street, and stopped.

He turned her to face the west. "The sun's setting." A yellowish-orange cast along the tops of the building.

"It's pretty."

"Yes, you are." He brushed a kiss on her forehead.

"You're sweet." She wrapped her arms around his neck and pressed her lips against his. A current of electricity seemed to buzz between them. A pleasant humming vibrated in her ears as she deepened the kiss.

They broke for air, and he tugged her hand. "Come on. You promised me fireworks."

That sounded like an innuendo for sex. Her lady parts quivered at the idea. They continued along the sidewalk to her condo.

Ivy unlocked her door. Marshmallow meowed and rubbed Ivy's legs. The cat turned, stared at Zander with its iridescent blue eyes, and hissed.

"Marshmallow, that's no way to treat company." She picked the feline up and scratched her under its chin. "Make yourself at home while I feed my cat. She's unbearable when she's hungry."

"I'm the same way." He waited on a button-tufted chair near the fireplace. She caught him staring at the open-beam ceiling with a staircase leading to her bedroom.

"Would you like something to drink?" Ivy asked from across a counter in the kitchen. "I can open a bottle of Chardonnay."

"Sounds good." He motioned to a four-part painting that fit together to show a man skateboarding. "I like this."

"Found it in a consignment shop. It took forever to mount the sections evenly." Darn it. She was rambling. "Here." She handed him the opened wine bottle and carried two fluted glasses. "Let's go upstairs" She pictured him laying on top of her king-sized bed. Should she even go there?

At the landing, she pointed to a door to the left. "The

balcony is right through my bedroom." She pulled back the drapes, opened the sliding glass door, and brought him to a rectangular area that overlooked the sloping street. An orange haze lined the horizon.

"I spend a lot of time out here." She set down the glasses on an end table, picked up a lighter, and attempted to light a tumbler candle. "Darn it."

"Allow me." With a flick of his thumb, he created a flame.

Did he have to be so cute? She reached for the bottle and filled her glass. "Want some?"

"Please."

She leaned closer. Her thigh brushed against his.

"I like your view from here." His gaze remained on her.

"The view's even better during the day. I often eat breakfast outside."

"Is that an offer for tomorrow?"

"Maybe." She tilted her head. "Did you say your shift's at nine?"

"It is." He picked up the bottle. "More."

Nodding, she sunk against the back cushion of the wicker loveseat, downing the drink, as her thoughts got a little fuzzy. "Are you trying to get me intoxicated?"

"Who me?" He finished his wine and placed his arm around her.

Nervous, she grabbed the throw and set it over the two of them. "I've never shared my balcony with anyone except Marshmallow."

"I feel privileged." He brushed a strand of hair behind her

ear. "Your eyes remind me of a chocolate fondue." The way his words rolled off his tongue made her feel all mushy inside.

"Thanks."

He took her glass from her hand and placed it on the end table. His mouth teased hers. Excitement coursed through her body as he deepened his response. And boy could he kiss.

He pulled away, and they watched the last rays of light fade from the sky. "We just spent another sunset together. Isn't that romantic?"

She anchored her arms around his neck and brought her lips to his, kissing him deep and hot until they were breathless. Her hands slipped under his T-shirt and enjoyed the feel of his firm muscles under her fingertips.

His fingers fiddled with her long silky hair. "I'm one lucky guy to be here with such a smart and smoking hot lady."

Her heart did a happy dance. "Oh, Zander." She snuggled into his arms.

He rubbed his hand along the back of her neck. Closing her eyes, she breathed in masculinity and sin. He kissed her softly, his tongue darted against hers, experimenting and tasting, growing bolder. The heat between them rose.

Crackling sounds boomed.

He pulled away, leaving her longing for more than the gold, silver, red, white, and blue fireworks exploding in the sky. She picked up her glass and sipped her wine.

"Thanks to you, we have our own private show," his voice got low.

"You're welcome." She surrendered to the heat of their joining mouths.

His hands roamed along her arms. Wickedly exotic tingles followed where he touched.

She bunched up his shirt, her fingertips massaging his back, craving for more skin, more contact, more him. As if he read her thoughts, he pulled his shirt over his head and continued kissing her. His hand drifted under her top to her bra.

She moaned.

"Let's take this inside," he said in a ragged voice as he stood, dragging her against him and giving her a long, luxurious kiss. Yearning for what he could offer, his kisses flamed her desire. All sense of logic frenzied.

He swept her into his arms, sliding her door open. They tumbled on top of her bed where the light had been left on. She peeled off her top and brought her mouth to his. His lips skimmed along her neck as one hand unlatched the hooks at the back of her bra. Then he feathered kisses at the vee between her breasts. She squirmed, craving more.

He sucked in a deep breath and kissed her again, softly, almost reverently, while exploring her nipples with his fingertips and teasing and taunting the tips. She nearly came undone. His hand roamed along her shoulders and down to her waist, reaching lower to undo the top snap of her shorts and zipping them down. She lifted her bottom. He stripped her down to her thong underwear.

"You're not playing fair." She undid his belt buckle, unzipped his pants, and could see the evidence of his large bulge and gave him a slight squeeze.

"You're driving me wild." He pushed off his pants. "I plan to savor and worship every part of you."

She nearly swooned.

His tongue swirled along the tip of her nipple, gave it a gentle bite and blew on it.

"Ohhh," she sighed.

He lifted his head from her breast and took the other nipple between his teeth, making her restless and needy. His hand drifted down to her mound, and he parted her legs and toyed with her clit as she squirmed.

When he dipped a finger inside her, she whimpered his name. Then he stroked her, his attention caused her hips to roll, and she dug her fingernails into his shoulders. He kept going. Her nerves were on fire. She clung to him as her orgasm spiraled, crying out his name as she undulated and quivered.

He stretched out next to her and caressed her cheek with his thumb. Her hands skated up his bare chest and traced his toned muscles. Her nerves were on fire as he stretched out next to her, caressing her cheek with his thumb and savoring her mouth. "I want you."

"Hurry," she moaned.

He got up. A condom wrapper crinkled as he rolled on

the latex and moved above her. His length pressed against her entrance. "Are you sure?" He gazed at her with such intensity.

"Yes," she said in a heady breath.

"Look at me." He settled between her, holding her hands above her head, and moved inside her slowly, steadily rocking into her, enjoying her at a leisurely pace. She skimmed his back with her nails. Her hips fell and moved in rhythm with his. A series of languid kisses accompanied his slow and steady strokes. Little by little, the pressure built.

Her breath became shaky as the intensity got faster and faster. She wrapped her legs around his waist, bucking underneath him. Every cell and fiber of her body tingled. He picked up the pace, each thrust harder, deeper, bringing her higher and higher, creating a friction of intense pleasure.

Ribbons of electricity arced through her. Sparks skated down her spine tearing away her control and causing a raging storm of heat as she rode on a cloud of ecstasy. And he kept on going. She bit his shoulder as he pushed her over the edge.

He rammed into her one more time, and she had another mind-blowing release that left her soaring.

"Wow," she whispered as the ecstasy faded and she came down.

"You're incredible." Turning to the side, he kept her in his arms. He reached down and ran his fingertips over the rose on her ankle. "Your birthmark feels similar to my heart emblem." He took her hand and had her outline the heart on his wrist. "Gives us something in common. Mine comes with special powers."

"You're crazy."

"You make me that way." His mouth anchored hers, and he kissed her. "But I'm not complaining."

Spent in the best of ways, her pulse beating wildly, she scrutinized the gorgeous man in her bed and hoped she could trust him not to crush her heart.

CHAPTER 22

Ivy woke with her head on Zander's shoulder and her arm across his waist. Her core quivered recalling the countless times he'd pleasured her with amazing, phenomenal, hot and heavy sex.

Why had she slept with him? The alcohol had weakened her inhibitions, but she couldn't blame everything on too much drinking. Their casual relationship just changed which scared her something fierce. He would be leaving at some point. Talk about messed up.

But she could handle this. It was just sex.

She couldn't resist running her fingertips along his abs. He stirred but didn't wake. To be honest, she longed to make love with him right now. After a long dry spell, he was definitely worth the wait.

Not that she'd slept with many men. She could count the

number on one hand. Besides, men always left, so she might as well accept this as truth.

If only he hadn't called her his lady.

His eyes fluttered open. His bow-shaped lips lifted in a half-smile. "Morning, gorgeous." A wave of blonde hair fell onto his forehead as he tenderly kissed her. He slipped his hand behind her head.

Her lips parted in anticipation, lost in his seductive tantalizing ways. His tongue stroked her lower lip. His mouth caused a bolt of electrifying desire through her entire being.

Her mouth tingled from a simple kiss. Hardly simple! His kisses were flaming hot. She matched him kiss for kiss until they ran out of breath. His fingers trailed to her throat and lower. Her hands were all over him. She craved him with a hunger that built with each caress. And then they were making love. Slow at first, in no time he had turned up the heat, setting her senses on fire, her internal embers stoked her higher and higher. A deliciously wicked sensation shot through her, exploding into an orgasm that rocked her soul. Moments later, he had his own release.

After a minute or two, he rolled to her side and pushed a strand of hair out of her eyes. "I'm starving."

She laughed.

"I'm a dude. We think with our stomachs." He kissed her cheek.

The cat bounded into the room and jumped onto the bed, hissed at him, and trotted out.

"What's up with him?"

"You mean her? Marshmallow gets a little testy when she's hungry. You two may have that in common."

"Hey, I'm never testy." He reached for her hand.

"Never? What about the last time you missed a triple kickflip?"

He gave one of those laughs that went deep. "You got me."

She grabbed a silk robe hanging on the back of her vanity's chair, covered her body, and tied the sash. "If you want breakfast, you'll have to join me in the kitchen." She walked to the door, adding an extra sway to her hips. Sex this morning sure lifted her spirits.

Her cat meowed, and she filled her bowl. Then she got out milk and eggs from the refrigerator.

"What are you making?" He stood behind her, wrapping his arms around her waist.

"French toast." She wiggled her bottom against him.

His stomach rumbled, and he stepped back. "What can I do to help?"

"Set the table. Plates are in the cupboard." She motioned to her right. "Silverware is right below." She cracked an egg, added milk, cinnamon, and vanilla, dipped bread into the batter, and set the slices into a pan. "There's OJ in the fridge if you'd like any. Would you mind pouring me a glass?"

"For you, Ivy, I'll do anything." His voice came out deep and husky, making it hard for her to concentrate.

Flipping the bread, she gazed at him sitting at her kitchen table like he belonged. She could get used to having him around like this. One night with him, and she was a goner.

Seeing him in her kitchen only reinforced their special connection. She brought the pan to the table and gave them each two slices of French toast.

"Besides being a badass paralegal, athlete and a fantastic cook, is there anything you can't do?"

Her heart did a little flip. "I'm a firebrand like the law firm where I work."

CHAPTER 23

Wednesday, July 8th

Zander walked out of the Caribou Board Shop whistling because he'd be meeting Ivy at a Japanese restaurant in about an hour. The only downside, her friends would be there. With a crazy, busy schedule the last couple of days, he hadn't seen her since he left her place on Monday morning. He hoped things between them didn't get awkward now that they'd had sex.

He'd been told that physical contact on Earth was off-limits. Yet he'd gone ahead and slept with a mortal. He should feel guilty. He should have at least a smidgen of remorse, but he didn't. In fact, Moosehead Lake had turned out to be a marvelous place—with Ivy an added bonus.

How things had changed in the last two months. His life had been planned out with Cami … until she jilted him for a human. Now, he had fallen into the same situation. Fate certainly had a wry sense of humor.

Skateboarding to the corner of Cardinal Way, he spotted the florist shop. Flowers said he'd like their relationship to continue. Too bad he hadn't bought her a set of wheel bearings or trucks at the board shop. Shit, he shouldn't be overthinking this. As a Cupid, he should be a master at romance. He knew the signs when a couple needed a love boost or the proper angle to shoot his arrow and hit his mark, but as far as mushy stuff, well … flowers would have to do. He walked inside and looked around.

Red roses represented love. They were lovers. Not quite the same thing.

"May I help you?" the male clerk asked.

"I'd like something for my lady." He picked up a mixed bouquet. "She likes pink."

"That's one of my favorites. The scattering of fragrant pink carnations with classy peonies and miniature roses should make your gal smile."

"That's what I'm counting on." He handed the clerk his Visa card. Then he headed east one block and entered the restaurant.

Rick waved him over to a table at the side of the room. And then he saw Ivy. She wore her hair loose, cascading down to her waist. He couldn't help but stare as he handed Ivy the flowers. "These reminded me of you."

"That's sweet." A blush crept up her cheeks.

He sat next to her and slid his arm along the back of her chair.

"Peonies are always a good choice," Sammy said.

"Care for some Sake?" Ivy picked up a ceramic pitcher.

"Absolutely." The awkwardness disappeared as he sipped the drink with a hint of fruit flavor.

"Sorry, I'm late." Penelope slid in the empty chair next to Rick. "What'd I miss?"

"Zander gave Ivy flowers," Sammy gushed. "Isn't that romantic?"

"It is." Penelope smiled at Zander. "How'd the interview go?"

"Great." $1000 a week plus benefits sounded fantastic to Zander. On a good week at Caribou, he'd made half that. The job description said he'd be running tournaments, coaching clinics and giving lessons. As long as he'd be staying on Earth, the position might be a good choice.

"You gonna take the job?" Sammy asked.

"I'm considering it." He dipped a mushroom spring roll in hot mustard sauce and popped it into his mouth.

"You anxious to replace me?" he asked Penelope.

"Nobody could ever replace you. Zander is one of a kind. Right, Ivy?"

"Sure is."

He gave her a chaste kiss while longing to get her alone.

"When are you moving in with Rick?" Sammy asked.

"Friday." In a few days, he'd be living a couple of blocks

from Ivy, and he really liked that idea. The trolley ride to the state park had gotten old

"Need any help moving your things?" Rick asked.

"Nope. I travel light." All he had were a few clothes and some odds and ends. For someone who had the best of everything, he didn't mind his meager Earthly belongings.

All evening, Ivy blushed whenever she gazed at him. Did she hope he'd go home with her because he'd be perfectly fine with that? Women were confusing. If only he had the power to read minds.

"I've got to help in court tomorrow and better get going," Ivy told the group. "The rest of the week will be crazy busy."

"Mind if I escort you home?" Zander whispered in her ear.

"Not at all."

"See you later," Sammy said as they headed out.

"I always do." Ivy waved to her friends, and she and Zander boarded down the street.

With her pink cap on backward and ponytail flying as she moved, she could easily pass for a teenager. In less than five minutes, they arrived at her condo. He pressed her against the door and brought his mouth to her lips. "I've missed you," he said, deepening the kiss.

She pulled back. "As have I, but—"

"You have to get up early." Meaning he wouldn't be invited inside.

"And you're moving Friday. What time do you get off on Saturday?"

"Six." He pushed a strand of hair behind her ear.

"Perfect. Would you like to come over for dinner?" A grin graced her face, and her eyes sparkled.

"I'd be honored." He pulled her into his arms and kissed her for the longest time.

CHAPTER 24

Saturday night

Zander knocked on Ivy's condominium door with a bottle of champagne in hand. He hadn't seen her since Wednesday and couldn't wait to have her alone to himself.

"Hey." Ivy opened the door, wearing a short off the shoulders dress. "Come on in."

He couldn't resist giving her a long luxurious kiss.

"What's the champagne for?"

"I decided to take the archery position."

"You're sticking around Moosehead?"

"For the time being."

Her smile faded for a flash, and he wished he could say he'd be staying forever, but sooner or later he'd go back to his former life. A savory aroma filled the air. "Something smells good."

"Island style teriyaki bowls. I'm almost done. Go ahead and have a seat at the table."

"What can I do to help?" He followed her into the kitchen, stood behind her, and nuzzled the back of her neck.

"Grab a couple of fluted glasses from the cupboard."

"Or I could stay right here and help you." He wrapped his hands around her waist. "I like this view."

"You're incorrigible." She removed his hands from around her.

"Maybe, but that's one of the reasons you like me."

"You're distracting. Go away and let me cook, or I'll end up burning the special meal I have for you," her voice came out sassy.

"Okay, I'll leave." He opened the cupboard and took out two crystal glasses. He watched her work, itching to pull her into his arms and run his fingers through her long locks. "Want me to open the champagne?"

"Sure."

He'd never opened a bottle without magic, but how hard could it be? Unwrapping the foil, he struggled to untwist the metal cage, set it on the table, and the cork popped off. Liquid flowed. He grabbed a glass, filled it, and quickly filled the other.

Ivy threw him a towel. "Too much bubbly for you, huh?"

He covered the bottle and set it down in the sink. "Don't you worry. There's still plenty left for us." Wiping his hands, he couldn't resist kissing her cheek, grabbing the bottle, and placing it in the center of the table.

Ivy set a plate in front of him and picked up her glass. "To new ventures," she toasted, and they clicked glasses. "Brutus is smart to hire you. After the flashy tricks you did at the tournament, I imagine there will be lots of folks who will ask for lessons."

"Maybe." The tricks he did were nothing compared to the stunts he'd done at archery competitions in Cupid's Corner. Shooting from over his shoulder or adding a line of glittering gold as his arrow hit dead center—tricks that received thunderous applause from the crowd. And one of his favorites had been flying up in the air and doing a triple flip. He missed having wings—he *really* missed flying. While skateboarding had its own advantages, it couldn't compare to having a pair of wings at his disposal. As much as he adored Ivy, he missed his Cupid position. Eventually, he'd end up breaking her heart, and that bothered him. In less than two months, he'd made himself a pretty sweet life. And right now, he had Ivy all to himself.

Her hand brushed his leg, and a blush crept up her cheeks. The innocent reaction was a far cry from the naughty thoughts that kept popping in his head—ones that required her naked and in bed.

"You all right?" She smiled at him.

He cleared his throat. Slices of pineapple, red and green peppers, onions, and zucchini were set on top of the rice. He took a bite, and the sweet and tangy flavors exploded on his tongue. "Delicious." She'd cooked this dinner for him. In Cupid's Corner, women could make anything with magic.

Here, they could order take-out or microwave a frozen dinner. Cooking took skill. A skill that Zander hadn't bothered mastering. It looked way too complicated.

"Glad you like it." She picked up her glass. "What else should we toast?"

"That … I'm sharing another night with a smart and stunning woman." He almost said that destiny led me to you, but he wasn't exactly sure if fate played any part in their meeting. All he knew was if he had to be stuck on Earth, he would've been bored if he hadn't met her.

"What a corny line," a short laugh escaped.

"And you love it." That line had worked on other females in the past. Of course, Ivy would call his bluff. Picking up his fork, he took another bite. "Is this a Japanese dish?"

"Islander." She flipped her hair behind her shoulders. "My grandmother taught me the recipe the last time I visited Rhapsody Island." She had mentioned the island located in the Bahamas before.

"What's it like?"

"As a child, I remember thinking the rainbow of vibrant colors made the place seem magical." Her eyes brightened. "My grandmother said the island was enchanted."

If Ivy believed in magic, would she believe him if he said he was a Cupid? Knowing her analytical mind, he doubted she'd consider the notion without him being able to prove it. Someday, his powers would be restored. "How old were you?"

"Young. The next time I went back, I must've been about

eight or nine. My mom sent my brother and me for a summer vacation. When I got older, I realized Mom wanted alone time with her newest husband." She held up three fingers.

"I'm guessing you and your brother helped in the kitchen with your grandmother." He enjoyed a delicious slice of pineapple.

"During the day, we went to the beach, and my grandfather and the locals taught us to surf."

"Surfing at eight. That must've been awesome." He'd like to try. "Does your grandmother still live on Rhapsody?"

"She does. We talk at least once a week. I promised her I'd visit, but it's been three years. Something always seems to come up." She rolled her eyes.

"You should go soon."

"Actually, I'm visiting her in a little over a month. Have you done much traveling?"

"I've been to Oregon and Washington along with Canada and Mexico." He'd been all over the world, including several different islands near Tahiti and the Bahamas, but that wouldn't fit for his cover story that he helped in the family factory. "I have to admit Moosehead turned out to be a great vacation."

"Moosehead has its charm," she said softly.

"It sure does." He winked at her, picked up the champagne bottle, and emptied the contents into both their glasses.

"Ready for dessert?"

He'd liked to sample a few more of her kisses. "Sure. Can I help?"

"You could grab the dishes and rinse them off in the sink." She sashayed by him into the kitchen.

Once he rinsed the dishes, he came behind her. "What'd you make?" His arms anchored around her waist, and he pulled her back to him and feathered kisses along her neck.

"Key lime pie." She cut a piece and set it on a plate.

He turned her to face him with her butt pressed against the counter. "I'd rather have you." He cupped her face. His mouth grazed hers as he got lost in the essence of Ivy.

"Not yet." She pushed him away. "You up for a movie?"

"Sure." That meant she'd be sitting next to him.

"Here's some aluminum foil. Cover the food while I slice the pie."

"Whatever you say, Ivy," he gave her a mock salute. The sooner he finished the task, the sooner he could be making out with her again. "What should we watch?" He didn't care as long as whatever movie they picked enhanced the mood.

They moved to the couch, and she clicked on the TV and flipped through romance. "You okay with *How to Lose A Guy in 10 Days?"*

He had seen this movie on a streaming cloud in college. "Sure."

She clicked the remote to start the movie. Then she shook a can of whipped cream and swirled it on top of the pie. "I thought we could share." She forked yellow pie into his mouth.

A sweet and tart custardy flavor sang through his taste buds. "Mmm."

"My turn." He picked up his fork and fed her a bite.

She reguarded him with her dark sultry eyes. "You're staring. Do I have whipped cream on my lips?" She ran her tongue along her mouth.

And his body stirred. "Let's see." Taking the plate out of her hand, he set it on the coffee table. Unable to resist touching her, he traced his finger over her velvety mouth. "You're so pretty." He lifted her onto his lap.

Her arms looped around his shoulders. The simple feel of her lips seemed to sear heat. Her mouth opened, inviting him in. When their tongues tangled, a jolt of desire scorched up the intensity. Holy Hades, he desired her something fierce.

Her hands moved under his shirt, and she tugged at the fabric.

He took it off.

She flicked warm kisses along his pecs and edged up his neck, licking and tasting before meeting back to his lips. The brush of her tongue and teeth drove him crazy.

An unexpected moan escaped from him. He pushed the elastic top down on her dress, exposing a sexy hot-pink strapless bra. Swallowing hard, he gazed at her body reverently, worshiping her cleavage as he ran his thumb across the shallow dip. His fingers undid the latch in the front. Her perky breasts tumbled out. "Have I told you that you're perfect?"

"No," she sighed.

He nibbled and explored, tracing one tip, then the other until he heard an impatient whimper. His mouth found the nipple, and she squirmed. He blew to make the tip harden, and she moaned as he encircled the other, squeezing and toying with her.

She rewarded him with a gasp. Her hand dipped into the waistband of his pants, undoing the top button and unzipping the zipper.

He pulled them both into a standing position and lifted her dress off her, allowing him to examine her lacy bikini underwear. Gorgeous legs, toned abs, slim waist, and those delightful breasts.

He brought his thumb under her chin and leaned down to kiss her hungrily, thoroughly, drowning in her intoxicating response. She matched him kiss for kiss. His palms skimmed over her ribs, hips, thighs, pushed down her panties, parting her legs and inserting his finger. He smiled, finding her wet and responsive.

Her hand slipped under the waistband of his boxers and encircled his cock. "I want—" She cupped him and rubbed his length.

Surprised, he nearly shot to the ceiling or might have if he had wings. His lungs were starved for oxygen as he sucked in a deep breath. "What do you want?"

"You."

He fumbled inside his pants' pocket, struggled to get the condom out of his wallet, dropped his jeans on the floor with his boxers. His hands were shaking as he tried to unwrap the foil.

"I'll do it." She nabbed the condom and had it on him in seconds. The feel of her hand on his cock driving him wild. He pressed her back on the couch and positioned himself between her legs. Urgency and need swept through him, but he longed to please her.

He entered her, watching this beautifully responsive woman. He inched in, keeping their tempo slow at first, building, stopping, building. Sparks seemed to arc from their connection as if he were in a realm filled with pleasure that kept intensifying. Her body tensed, and he dragged her pleasure out.

He called her name, his voice husky, slowing the pace, wanting her to crave him and crave for more. He kissed her, her little moans urging him on. He pulled out, teased her lips with his mouth.

"More, faster." She squeezed the tip with her core.

His thrusts became deeper, harder, the crescendo about to erupt, her body quivered, and he peaked, riding the tide of ecstasy together.

He collapsed on top of her, sated and totally content.

CHAPTER 25

Sunday afternoon, Ivy unlocked the gate and brought Zander into her condo's pool. After last night and this morning, water should soothe her well-satisfied body

"Is it usually this empty here?"

"Most days." Another reason why she liked this complex. "People prefer to be out on the lake when it's warm."

"Works for me." He threw his towel on a lounge chair and stripped off his T-shirt. His muscles rippled on his chest, the same chest she'd explored with her hands and her mouth. Her pulse quickened.

His eyes scanned her body as she stripped off her dress to her bikini. She experienced a sudden bout of shyness. Utter lunacy since he'd just seen her naked last night.

He let out a wolf whistle, which broke the tension.

She laughed.

"I know a sexy lady when I see one." He strutted toward the deep end and dove in.

Water glistened off his body, and he kept swimming laps. Her core quivered watching him. She was in deep water with this guy and knew better than to give him her heart. Too late. It hammered hard in her chest.

"The water's great. Come on in." His grin widened.

No way could she resist those dimples, that face, and the whole package. Still, she took her time walking to the steps and waded in slowly until the water reached her shoulders.

Like a magnet, Zander swam next to her and pulled her into his arms. Even though she could stand, her legs swayed. He deepened the kiss. She reveled in the feel of Zander's mouth as he held her in his arms

"Race you to the deep end and back." She took off. Competitive, she swam hard.

He caught up to her at the pool's edge. Shot off toward the shallow end. "You might be good for a lap. Think you have the stamina for ten laps?"

And they raced. Gliding along, the water sheathed her in coolness. She closed out the world, cupped her hand, and synchronized her flutter kicks. Reaching the edge, she flipped under to turn and kept going. She didn't slow until she reached the area deep enough where she could stand.

Zander came up from behind. He turned her and pulled her into his embrace. With her hands on his shoulders, her ragged breathing matched his. Her body mashed against his growing length, and she raked her fingers through his hair.

His eyes darkened to midnight blue, rousing heat deep within her.

And then he smiled. Handsome. Impish. Oh, so addictive.

His mouth moved lazily over hers, creating the most exquisite torture with his tongue. Her breasts ached. Her belly quivered and a throb pulsed between her thighs. Even after all the times they made love, desire for him consumed her.

The gate squeaked open, and she gasped, "We've got company."

A woman with a little girl wearing an inflatable flamingo around her waist walked in. "Hello," she called. "I hope we're not disturbing you."

Another few minutes and—no telling what compromising position they might have been in. Ivy glanced over at Zander.

"Not at all." He walked toward the steps. "We were just about to leave."

"Mommy's taking me swimming," the child said.

"Sarah loves the water," the mother explained.

"I like your flamingo." Zander gave an endearing smile. He stepped out of the pool and strolled over to his chair to get his towel.

"Flamingos are pink. I like pink," the girl said.

"So do I." Ivy got out, noting Zander's eyes sweeping across her body. She ran her tongue over her bottom lip. He watched her every movement as she wrapped in her towel and grabbed her things. "Ready," she asked him.

"More than you'll ever know. Have a nice swim." He waved to the mother and child and ushered her out the gate.

"That was awkward." His serious expression matched his rigid stance.

"Definitely."

"The problem is that your irresistible." He placed his arm around her. "Next weekend, I have to help out at an archery meet in Raccoon Junction. I'm hoping you'll go with me." His eyes softened, and he leaned over, kissed her cheek.

"Okay."

"I'll pick you up Friday night around seven." He kissed her once more.

She was falling hard for him.

~

SUNDAY, 11 a.m., Racoon Junction

IVY FINALLY HAD LET her guard down and lived in the present. She and Zander had a playful, competitive friendship. Their chemistry had been electrifying from the beginning. Resisting him—impossible.

Friday night, he set her off with countless orgasms. Saturday after he'd finished working the meet, she had greeted him in a lacy teddy. He growled and took her against the door. By Sunday morning, she'd lost count of the ways they'd pleasured each other. Not that she was complaining.

Zander had rocked her world in the best of ways and not just because of the sex. He liked doing risky things, pushing the envelope. If she hadn't met him, she doubted she would have gone paddle boarding. And now she waited in line with Zander on Raccoon Junction's Ziplining platform.

"You okay?" Zander asked.

"I can't believe I'm going to fly down that cable." She watched the woman four spots in front of her take-off and scream.

"Are you afraid?" Zander whispered into her ear.

Not about to admit being a bit apprehensive, she glanced down and took in the view of the entire valley. "No." As she moved closer to the edge, her stomach did a funny flip as a slight panic formed in her throat. The bottom appeared to be a long way down.

"I'd rather use wings," Zander said.

"Wings? Are you saying you'd rather jump off the edge and paraglide?" With the ground eons of yards away, paragliding didn't appeal to her one iota.

"Sounds fun. We'll try that next time."

"You need to step in and shimmy the device up to your waist," a worker instructed. "Fix the waist. Not too tight but snug."

She adjusted the legs on the harness.

"I'm going to pass the lanyard through the anchor point, loop it in place, and click it to the cable." He attached the clip for her. "Sit in it and see if everything feels secure."

She looked up. The slope of the cable seemed to go on

forever, and if it broke, she'd be a goner. Now that she made it to the takeoff junction, zip lining might not be such a great idea.

"Go ahead when you're ready," the worker said.

Okay, she could do this. She stepped off the platform and whooshed at a slant downward, breathing in fresh air. Watching the horizon. The trees and flowers could pass for blurred paint. It seemed similar to riding a roller coaster except her only attachment to the cable was a tiny lanyard.

"Waaa. Whooo," Zander shouted.

She checked behind her. Big mistake because she wobbled a little. Focusing forward, she concentrated on the air swooshing along her arms and face and neck, tugging her ponytail backward. By the time she spotted the landing site, a hint of disappointment hit her from deep within. As she flew across the sky, she had been carefree. Her feet touched the ground. She unclipped her line, took off her helmet, and turned to watch Zander.

His smile couldn't be any wider as he landed. "Wow!"

"It was exhilarating." Ivy stepped closer.

"And we got to share this together." He pulled her into his arms and kissed her. "Have I told you how incredible you are?"

"Not lately, but you certainly showed me."

"I aim to please." His eyes became dark blue topaz. "Once we get back to your place, I plan to show you again … and again."

Heat pooled into her core, and her face got hot.

"You're cute when you blush." He took her hand, and they walked inside the building to turn in their equipment.

Her stomach grumbled. "I'm starving. You promised we'd stop for burgers on the way home."

"If that's what you want." He kissed the top of her head.

His low tone made her all gushy inside. Deep down in the recesses of her mind, her insecurity surfaced. Handsome men can't be trusted. She pushed the insecurity away.

CHAPTER 26

A week later, Zander left the board shop and skated down Caribou Avenue to meet Ivy for dinner. Just thinking about her made him smile. He liked the way she'd ribbed him when he failed a skateboarding trick or told him to knock it off when he tried to show off. Mistakes didn't seem to matter on Earth, nor did they matter to her. She didn't care if she fit in, wore her cap backward, and even though she owned a car, she preferred taking the trolley or skateboarding.

With Cupid's Corner like a distant memory, he wouldn't mind staying indefinitely in Moosehead. His future had changed in the past two months since Cami dumped him. He'd been enamored with the idea of their status together. Ivy made him feel special.

It wasn't love. It couldn't be because humans were off-limits, but if he could choose his ideal mate, it would be her.

Still, if anyone from his realm learned he slept with her, his family's stellar reputation might be tarnished. Sleeping with a human was considered wrong … even forbidden … but after meeting Ivy and experiencing their undeniable chemistry, he figured plenty of Cupids had secret affairs with humans. His relationship with her could never be the forever kind. A sinking sensation filled his gut. At some point, he and Ivy would part ways.

"Is that you, Zander?" A familiar voice echoed in his ear. A winged figure flittered inches from his face.

Zander stopped his board, flipped it in his hand, and stared at a Cupid friend from his hometown. "Hey, Quin. What are you doing in Moosehead?"

Oh shit! He wasn't ready for this. After almost two months, he'd prefer to spend another night or two with Ivy.

"I had some time to kill before my assignment at Moosehead Lodge and decided to check out the town. Why are you impersonating a human? Last I heard, you were vacationing in Lover's Landing."

"It's a long story." One he didn't care to tell.

"I've got a few minutes. You missed an extra month. Your uncle had me cover some of your shifts, so I figure you owe me an explanation."

"You heard about Cami, right?" His uncle had given him a month to get his act together but said he'd extend his time off for longer if needed.

"I did. She's married to a human. Sorry, bro," Quin said. "Guess it makes sense you'd be a little off, but I don't get how you ended up in Moosehead?"

"I had an assignment and assumed it'd be a good idea to change into a human form and get drunk. The next day, my magical abilities disappeared, and I didn't remember to pack any extra vials of dust."

"That's hilarious." Quin laughed. "You're supposed to be everyone's role model, yet you forgot one of the biggest rules ... always pack four vials of dust in case of an emergency."

"Pretty lame." It suddenly dawned on Zander that with a little help, he could go back to his accustomed lifestyle. He never truly belonged here. The idea saddened him. "Think you could loan me one of your vials?"

Quin reached into his pocket and handed Zander a glass tube.

"I'd appreciate it if you didn't mention my mishap to anyone."

"What happens here will stay with me. Never know when I might need a favor myself."

"You've got it." Zander held the tiny vial in his hand and placed the glass tube inside a pocket. Checking his phone and seeing it was close to six p.m., he still had a couple hours of sunlight left to ride a beam back to Cupid's Corner.

"To be honest, several of the Cupids assumed after you and Cami split up, you went to the Forest of Enchantment. We had bets on how long you'd stay there. If you come back today, I'll win the pot." Quinn smirked. "Were you stuck in Moosehead the whole time?"

"It wasn't bad." Not after he and Ivy got close.

"If you say so." Quinn shook his head. "Bet you can't wait to get back home."

Home where his life would be normal again. Home to what made sense. Home to his predestined career where he'd enjoy his family's elite status. He should be ecstatic but wasn't.

Quin checked his wrist emblem. "Gotta go."

"Thanks again. You're a lifesaver." He'd better head for the apartment he shared with Rick and collect any Cupid world items, but first he had to see Ivy and call it quits.

IVY STIRRED her straw around her soda as she waited in the pizzeria. She'd been lucky to get a table with a view of the lake. A speedboat zipped off in the distance. Water skiing might make an entertaining weekend with Zander.

She glanced at her phone. 7:00 p.m. He should've arrived thirty minutes ago. Inventory must've taken longer than expected.

She texted. *Where RU?*

Nothing.

Probably misplaced his phone … again. She checked the entrance and spotted him.

He waved but didn't smile as he sat in a chair across from

her. "Sorry I'm late." He picked up the menu and glanced at it, which didn't make sense since he always ordered the veggie pizza.

Instead of tiptoeing around whatever bothered him, she asked, "Is something wrong?"

"I have to go home."

"For how long?"

"For good. My family needs me."

"I assumed you'd be sticking around for the next month or two."

"That had been the plan. It's complicated." He still wouldn't look her in the eye. "Ivy, you're a great person."

"But you're breaking up with me."

"It's not what I want. You know long-distance relationships don't work." He clenched his jaw, his neck corded. "I should have never started this relationship knowing that I'd have to leave. Ivy, I'm sorry, really sorry."

"So am I." Tears threatened to spill. No way could she stick around there and let him see her fall apart. "Goodbye. Have a good life." She threw down a twenty and rushed out the door, refusing to glance back at him. He broke up with her. A hurt built deep within her. How could he do this to her?

Skating up Caribou Avenue, she passed the bicycle and gift stores and the skate shop where Zander sold her those pink shoes. She should have turned around when she first saw him, should never have gone paddleboarding, never gone out with him, never trusted him. What an idiot she had been. He was no different than other men in her life.

She got to her condo. Marshmallow meowed as she walked in. She poured food into her bowl. "You hissed at Zander. I should've listened to your instincts," she said to the cat. Marshmallow gobbled her kibble.

She flopped onto the couch—the same couch where they'd made love. Dammit. He's such a jerk. She FaceTimed Sammy and Penelope.

Penelope clicked in first. "Hi."

"Hey, guys. What's up?" Sammy chimed in.

"Zander just broke up with me." The words hit her like a bomb just detonated in her head. His smitten behavior had all been an act.

"I don't get it. He acted excited to see you tonight," Penelope said.

"He said he had to go home."

"For how long?" Sammy asked.

"He's not coming back ... ever. He said long-distance relationships don't work." Ivy sobbed. Dammit. She never cried.

"Hold tight," Sammy said. "I'm coming right over."

"Me, too. I'll bring the tequila."

Ivy sunk into the couch. Marshmallow climbed into her lap. "How could I have been so gullible?"

Her cat meowed as if agreeing.

The doorbell rang.

"It's open," she called.

Sammy rushed inside and hugged her. "I can't believe Zander dumped you."

"Well, he did."

Penelope came in holding a large paper sack which she put on the counter. "Let's start with tequila shooters. Then, I'll make margaritas."

"The tequila tradition," Sammy said.

Tequila shooters for a horrendous day. Penelope started the ritual after her live-in boyfriend decided to move across the country without her. Sammy came next when her husband went behind her back and bought a brand-new jeep when she'd begged for a Camaro. And now it was Ivy's turn. Tears filled her eyes.

Ivy got up and grabbed three shot glasses from a cabinet. Sammy poured salt into a dish. Penelope cut a lime in half, twisted the rim of the glass with lime, salted the rim, and cut the other half into three wedges. Ivy opened the bottle and poured. Each woman grabbed a drink and a wedge.

"One, two, three, go," Penelope said.

The sharp taste of tequila burned her throat as it went down. She grabbed a lime wedge, sucking hard.

"What can we do to help?" Sammy asked.

"Slap me if I ever consider dating again. I knew better than to trust Zander. Why am I so dumb?"

"You're not dumb. Did Zander ever say he wanted a serious relationship?" Penelope poured another shot in her glass.

"He called me his lady." And she bought right into it.

"Not the same thing. Bottoms up," Penelope said.

The burn wasn't as fiery this time.

"There's no doubt that he liked you, Ivy. You could see it in his eyes. I bet he would have stayed with you if he could." Always the romantic, Sammy's words didn't comfort her.

Instead, they made her cry.

"Forget him." Sammy placed her hand on Ivy's shoulder. "He doesn't deserve you."

"Let's switch to margaritas." Penelope turned on the blender. In no time, the three of them were sitting on the couch, drinking from stemmed cocktail glasses.

"How's it going with Rick?" Ivy asked to divert the conversation away from Zander.

"Good, except sometimes I get this weird feeling. One I can't quite figure out."

"What do you mean?" Sammy eyed Penelope.

"I've had a crush on him since we first met."

"I get it. Zander used me as his vacation girlfriend." Ivy sniffled. "I've been such a fool." And she was tired of the game. The rejection stung deep within Ivy's soul.

CHAPTER 27

Zander's chest tightened as he recalled the sadness etched in Ivy's face. As he walked into his apartment, he felt like a first-class heel. Hopefully, his human friend would be out, and he wouldn't have to tell him about the breakup. At least he had paid two months in advance.

"You okay," Rick asked from the couch.

"Not really. I have to go home."

"What's up?"

"It's a family thing. I'm grabbing a few things and need to get to the airport."

"I'll drive you there."

Moosehead's airport was reasonably close to a sunbeam. "Appreciate it." He went into his room, sifted through the drawers in his dresser, took his wallet and the clothes he'd worn into the Bison Tavern.

"Does Ivy know you're leaving?" Rick asked as they got into the car and started driving.

"She does." Except she didn't know the real reason. He never should have slept with her, but to be honest, he couldn't help himself.

"When you coming back?"

They arrived at the terminal. "I'm not … sure." Instead of saying never, he opened the door.

"Text when you're back in town."

"Will do. Thanks." He watched Rick drive off, rushed across the parking lot behind a cluster of tall trees, and sprinkled dust from the borrowed vial over his body. Changing into his Cupid form seemed odd. He'd gotten used to being bigger. His pulse pumped fast as he zoomed up the sunbeam toward his familiar life. He missed flying. He missed the sensation of unfurled wings pulling at his shoulder blades and their sparkly turquoise color glimmering in the sunlight.

In less than twenty seconds, he entered the heavenly realm.

Yes! He'd made it home.

From his calculations, it'd been eight weeks. He'd rather not admit he'd been on Earth this whole time especially after Ivy.

He arrived at his apartment on the fifth floor. It seemed like an eternity since he'd parted a cloud-covered door and furled his wings. Inside, he opened a window, breathed deeply, and gazed at the Fates River as it meandered toward Lake Aphrodite.

His stomach growled. He went into the kitchen, expecting to open up the fridge and see what was inside.

No fridge. No stove. No sink.

What?

His red wrist emblem shimmered. Obviously, his magic had been restored the moment he entered the heavenly realm. Flicking his fingertips cardinal-colored dust swirled. A platter of food appeared on the table. After months without magic, a thrill shot through him.

He sat in a chair and savored a piece of dragon fruit. It tasted sweeter than candy. Picking up a toasted baguette and brie cheese sandwich, he dipped it in a ceramic ramekin filled with spinach and artichoke sauce. Delicious. Swirling more dust, he drank Ambrosia from a fluted crystal glass. The liquid tickled as it went down his throat.

A bachelor pad. Magic at his fingertips. Home—where he belonged.

Something deep inside him felt off. He chalked the notion up to readjusting to this realm. Moosehead had been a vacation from his own reality. Yes, he'd had a good time but being a Cupid archer was his true calling.

He looked at a blueprint sitting on the table. The plans showed a new home on his family estate where he and Cami should be raising another generation of Eros'. He had envisioned at least two boys that resembled him. Two girls who inherited Cami's loveliness. A perfect life. One that most likely would have made him miserable.

If only Ivy fit into this world, but she didn't. And he never truly belonged on Earth. He needed to forget her and move on.

CHAPTER 28

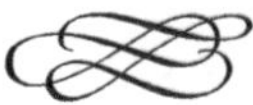

The next day, Zander called his mom.

"Where have you been? I've been worried," his mother said.

"I'm fine. How are you?"

"Better now that you're home. Cami had no right to crush your heart like she did."

"I'm over her." Cami was old news—because of one very sexy human. Not exactly the thing to bring up with his parents.

"I hope so. Someday you'll meet your true love," she sighed. "When are you going to stop by the house?"

"Soon."

"Come by for dinner on Sunday. Your brothers are in town. I'll make sure they attend with their families." Her voice held a don't-you-dare-argue tone.

"I'll do my best." Like he had a choice. As much as he wanted to see his family, the idea that they would be feeling sorry for him didn't sit well. "Gotta go. I'll call you tomorrow."

An hour later, Zander flew along Paramour Street, past the park, and floated down to the building on the corner. His hand felt empty without his skateboard. How ridiculous. He had wings now.

Close to noon, he might as well get something to eat at Passion's Pasta. He headed for a table near the back. Several yards to his right, two older women chatted at a corner table.

As he walked by, he heard one say, "Cami didn't deserve Zander."

"He should date my little Cherish," the other said.

Zander almost laughed. Cherish Lovelorn was not the brightest star in the sky. And he had no desire to be set up with anyone except ... an image flashed in his mind of Ivy. Her chocolate-colored eyes sparkling as she's tossing her silky waist-long ebony hair over her shoulder. Cursed Cyclops. He had to stop thinking about Idaho and ... Ivy.

"Hey, Zander." A strawberry blonde waitress stood by his table.

"Hello."

"Want the usual?" the waitress asked. "Fettuccini Alfredo with artichoke hearts."

"Absolutely." He read her name tag. Briar must've waited on him before, although he didn't remember her. Cute with a beaming smile and big blue eyes with fluttering long lashes. Apparently available. He could ask her out.

Too bad he didn't feel any spark. All Ivy had to do was glance at him, and his pulse raced faster than a unicorn's hooves galloping through the forest. Holy Zeus. He had to stop this nonsense.

"Hey Zander." His friend, Wynton, strutted up to the table.

"Have a seat." Zander motioned to sit across from him at the empty side and gave Briar his order.

"What are you doing back in Cupid's Corner?" His friend had accepted a job at the marina in Lover's Landing a few weeks before Zander went to Earth.

"I'm in town for a couple of days. Aunt April just gave me a promotion. Starting a week from Monday, I'll be the general manager." Wynton's eyes practically danced with excitement.

"Good for you."

"I'm living the dream. Testing the latest watercraft. Plenty of females on vacation ready to have fun in the sun."

Zander had his own share of fun on Earth. Too bad that part of his life was over.

"I'm staying aboard my aunt's houseboat while I'm here."

"You're not just living the dream; you're living like a prince."

"I still can't believe it. Last year, I barely scraped by." His friend grinned. "When's the wedding?"

"Not gonna happen. Cami married a human."

Wynton's eyes widened. "You're kidding?"

"You heard how her arrow hit the wrong target."

"No. Guess I've been out of town too long. What happened?"

"She was supposed to find her recipient human his soulmate ... decided she wanted the job."

"Sorry."

"Actually, I no longer care." Talking about the situation no longer made Zander's blood boil. He really was over her.

"To be honest, the two of you never seemed to have any spark."

In bed, he and Ivy fired like a combustible engine.

The waitress brought out their food. "Is there anything else you need?" Briar focused on Zander.

"Nothing at the moment." Wynton flashed her a smile

She sauntered away.

"She's hot and definitely into you." Wynton dipped a fry in ketchup. "You should ask her out."

"She's not my type." He *had* found an intriguing human. Not like he'd mention that.

"I bet you've already met someone else." Wynton laughed. "Do tell about your mystery Cupid."

"There's no one." Not in Cupid's Corner anyway.

"Well, I'm having a party Sunday. You should come."

"I'll think about it."

"I might even invite Briar." Wynton's brows scrunched together. "I planned to invite Belle and stopped by her place earlier today. She wasn't home. I've messaged her, but she hasn't answered. Any idea where she might be?"

"Can't help you. Been out of town."

"That's right. Being a Cupid archer keeps you busy on Earth."

"It does." He could tell him about his two-month stint, but now didn't seem like the right time.

"I'm not heading back to Lover's Landing until Tuesday. Hopefully, I'll connect with Belle before then." Wynton always had a thing for Belle, while she didn't seem to return the ardor.

"About the party. I'll have to leave by midnight." His assignment started at ten a.m. Monday.

"For a second, I assumed you'd become the male version of Cinderella, and your magical abilities disappeared at the stroke of midnight." Wynton let out a rip-roaring hoot.

"Good to see you haven't lost your sense of humor," Zander laughed.

CHAPTER 29

Zander fluttered along the quay and appreciated the sleek lines of the Lady Aphrodite. Bubblegum-colored with a white upper-decking, this was no houseboat but a luxury yacht.

On the bow, about a dozen female Cupids in short dresses line danced to the "Cupid Shuffle." Couples clustered along the bridge. Wynton's laughter came from the starboard side. Zander landed next to his friend who had his arm draped around a voluptuous redhead.

"You made it," Wynton said.

"Heard you and Cami broke up." The captain of his high school rowing team wore a beaming grin. The guy had always hoped to date her, but she turned him down flat.

"Yep." Ancient history.

"I'm glad she did." Briar, the waitress from the restaurant, stood to his right. Cute and bubbly, she wasn't coy about inching in close to him.

"So am I." Otherwise, he would never have met Ivy.

A server in a red tuxedo brought over a tray of shimmering pink drinks in hurricane glasses.

"Help yourselves to a Fabulous Fizzy." Wynton handed a glass to his date and took one for himself. "It's my favorite cocktail. Sweet with an unexpected kick."

Zander could use a kick to help him relax. The cocktail tasted like strawberry soda. Downing his drink, he soon found another in his hand.

"What's it like on Earth?" Briar asked.

"Imagine a king-sized version of this place but with a lot more people."

"Oh. I doubt I'd like the crowds." She had pretty azure-blue eyes.

He found himself longing to see dark chocolate ones. "It's not that different from here. My last assignment had a lake similar to Lake Aphrodite." An image of Ivy paddle boarding with water dripping off her body came to mind. He tried to shake it off.

"Have you ever talked with a human?" Wynton's date asked.

That question came from outer space. "No, but I've overheard plenty of conversations. Humans talk about sports, weather, trivial things just like here."

"It sounds exciting. I'd love to tag along." Briar put her hand on his shoulder.

"That'd be against the rules." So was kissing a human and … sex with a human.

"Devil" by Shinedown blasted from speakers. "I love this song. Dance with me." Briar led him toward the bow of the watercraft.

As he walked by the waiter, he snatched another drink, downed it, and set the empty glass on a table. He slow danced with Briar, line-danced with the crowd, did the Macarena. And as the night went on, he laughed, danced and drank, becoming more than a little buzzed and quite happy.

This was what he called living. Prestige. Dancing with a cute female. Then he spotted a dark-haired beauty who reminded him of Ivy. Fate was undoubtedly toying with his emotions.

A WARM BODY pressed against Zander.

"Ivy?"

He opened his eyes and spotted a miniature poodle sleeping on the same twin bed as he. Where in Hades was he?

The yacht. He'd partied hard. The last time he'd drank this much, he woke up in a Moosehead jail cell. This place was definitely an improvement. His head started to pound like a hammer hitting a nail.

Not good.

He glanced at his heart emblem. Nine-thirty a.m. His

assignment flashed. Holy Zeus. He had thirty minutes to get there on time. Why didn't his alarm go off?

He sat up and flicked his magical dust to create a hangover cure, downed the drink, changed clothes, fixed his hair, unfurled his wings, and headed across town to grab his bow and quiver from his apartment.

Ten minutes later, he zoomed through the forest, between two redwoods and slid down a sunbeam.

Being back to work, he had regained his purpose. Luckily, he'd memorized the couple's info on Saturday morning. He pinpointed the Oregon town of Romance twenty miles from the Idaho border, skidded to a stop on the roof of a hotel and checked the time.

Fourteen minutes late.

A woman stood under the eaves of the hotel's restaurant and talked on the phone. Her greyish-blue aura showed distress as she rubbed her belly. "We were having a nice breakfast until I told him—" she blubbered. "Said he had to go and walked out." The brunette paced toward Zander.

He sucked in a deep breath. He'd made love to Ivy countless times. Thank the gods, he had used protection. Impregnating a human—a colossal disaster.

Still, he couldn't help wondering what their cherubs might look like. The girls would have shiny black hair and dark eyes. The boys would be blond with blue eyes like him. Or maybe they might be a mix of both of them.

Okay, quit getting off track.

"His stuff's gone." The woman paced as she continued talking on her phone.

Zander's gut tightened. This assignment might last for the next day or two. At least this time he'd packed eight vials of magical dust.

"No, you don't need to come. My ride should be here any second." She gave a long, drawn-out sigh that ended with a hiccup. "Looks like the car just pulled up. Call you later." The woman walked to a lime green sedan parked along the curb and opened a door.

Zander followed her.

"April, wait," someone called. A tall, lanky guy ran up to her. "Hear me out."

Zander recognized the guy from the Cupid's Connection report. He took his bow off his shoulder, set his arrow, checked his aim and released his love-infused arrow into the guy's heart.

"Why should I listen?" the woman asked.

"Because I love you." He pulled her into his arms.

Problem solved. He didn't have another assignment until Wednesday. Maybe he should fly over and see Ivy. Scratch that. She didn't belong in his world. He headed up the sunbeam.

CHAPTER 30

A text chimed. Ivy snatched her phone, hoping the message came from Zander, not her best friend, Sammy. My god, she was pathetic. It'd been three weeks—twenty-one stinking days since the breakup. It pissed her off that she still thought about him. Like her mother, she caved when a handsome man doled out a little attention. Well, not anymore. Right now, she was full-on pissed.

Straightening the stack of papers on her desk, the song "I Hate Myself for Loving You" blared from a speaker on the wall.

How appropriate!

She shut down the work computer and pulled dark jeans and a black T-shirt out of her backpack.

I've gotta get out of here.

Once outside, she hopped on her board and zoomed

down the street. The thrill that usually filled her was gone. She recalled racing skateboards on this very street with Zander, and she'd won. He'd shrugged and gave her a kiss that could melt a snowman. Damn him.

Arriving at the Blue Birch Café, she flipped her board into her hand and spotted Sammy and Penelope waving from a booth along a wall of windows. Ivy scooted in next to Sammy.

"Wine," Sammy held up a decanter.

Ivy nodded.

"The station just hired a new dispatcher. He's cute." Sammy canted her head and gave her a wane smile.

"I'm through with men forever." Why did people assume she needed a man to be happy? She could manage just fine without one.

Sammy bit her bottom lip, obviously holding back a retort.

Penelope gave her an empathetic look.

"Knock it off, guys. I'm doing just fine." As long as they quit bringing up dating.

"You haven't been in the store for a while. We've got a new shipment of snowboards. There's a pink one with your name on it."

"Not into pink anymore. Do you have anything interesting in black?"

Sammy rolled her eyes.

"There's nothing wrong with black." Except, the dark color did nothing to brighten her spirits.

"You look better in pastels and brighter colors." One of Sammy's eyebrows quirked up. "You know, it's been forever since we went on a shopping spree. We should drive into Bison Valley."

"Add in a spa day, and I'm in. Saturday works for me." Penelope rubbed her hands together.

"Me, too. And I know you're off, Ivy. Please say you'll go?" Sammy pleaded.

"I'll think about it." A trip out of town did sound entertaining.

Penelope glanced toward the entrance and gasped. Zander strode straight for their booth. Her friends glared at him.

"Don't either of you dare leave me alone with him," Ivy said through clenched teeth. Yes-siree, her crappy day just got worse.

FOR THE LAST THREE WEEKS, Zander told himself he was happy. He worked at a job he loved. He helped couples restore their love lives. He made a difference.

Since everyone in Cupid's Corner knew about Cami, he had assumed that Cupid females would be empathetic or pity him now that he was officially single, not practically throw themselves at him when he went out to the local hangouts. Beautiful Cupids seemed to flock around him.

None of them captured his interest. None of them intrigued him. None of them could compete with Ivy.

And today he finally gave in to the inevitable—fate had thrown him and Ivy together for a reason. As unwise as their relationship had been, he had to see her again. He missed skateboarding next to her. He missed how her eyes sparkled when she gazed at him. He missed how she made him feel alive.

Nothing went as planned. His assignment took longer than he'd expected. Top that off with a wrong turn, and he arrived in Moosehead at well after seven. Thus, he didn't catch her at her office. He had gone to her condo, then to the pizzeria, Mexican restaurant, and now the café. His nerves rattled. Seeing Ivy and her friends glaring at him as he approached the table didn't sit well with him, but he was here, and he wasn't about to leave without making things right.

"What do you want?" Ivy said as he stood by the table, her eyes fired with fury.

"A minute of your time, alone."

"Whatever you have to say, you can say in front of my friends."

Holy Zeus. She even looked gorgeous when she scowled.

"Can't wait to hear what he says." Penelope folded her arms while Sammy nodded in agreement.

He'd blown it big time with Ivy. What could he say to make up for hurting her? Unused to being scrutinized like this, Zander swallowed hard. "Sorry I didn't call." He couldn't think straight.

"Why would you? You made it clear we were through," Ivy snarled.

"I've missed you."

"Like I care."

"Please give me another chance." He had no business being with Ivy, begging for forgiveness. Zander had never begged before.

"No thanks." Ivy wouldn't even look at him.

If he could just speak with her alone, he'd explain the whole truth. He couldn't explain anything with the disproving looks of this audience. His mind was nearly as frazzled as his nerves.

"I'm not buying into your bull. You need to leave." Ivy's voice held a venomous tone.

"What if I said I figured out a way for us to be together?"

"This is getting good." Penelope put her hands under her chin.

"Go on. What's your big plan?" Ivy asked without even a flicker of a smile.

"I could move back here … but cut back on my job in Heavenly. I mean … when I'm not …. on assignment … I would see you three … or four days a week." His idea sounded reasonable.

"You're too much," her voice seethed. "I never want to see you again, ever."

"You can't mean that." Zander couldn't believe how much Ivy's rejection hurt.

"That's your cue to split." Penelope glowered at him.

The restaurant's manager walked up to the table. "Is there a problem here?"

"Yes. This man needs to leave now." Sammy pointed her finger at Zander.

"All right, I'll go." His eyes lingered on Ivy before he turned away and left.

He could shoot arrows that infused love for people but could do nothing to help himself? He'd crushed the heart of the only woman that he cared about. He had to win her back.

Not an easy task considering she seemed to despise him.

CHAPTER 31

Instead of going to Cupid's Corner, Zander headed for Lover's Landing. His longtime friend would help sort out his issues with Ivy. He landed on a dock outside the largest houseboat. "Wynton, are you home?"

"Be right up," his friend called and stepped onto the galley. "What brings you here on a Friday night?"

"It's complicated," Zander heard himself groan.

"All females are." His friend motioned for him to board.

"You've got that right."

"Who's the woman?"

"No one you know." Zander leaned his arm against the deck's railing.

"This oughta help." Wynton floated a snifter of amaretto into his hand. "You wanna talk about it?"

He nodded. "Is there anyone else on board? What I'm about to explain is confidential."

"It's just me."

"I'm hooked on a human named Ivy," Zander blurted.

"Cami must've really messed with your head for you to do that."

"Cami has nothing to do with this." Except he wouldn't have been drinking if Cami hadn't gotten married the night before, and he wouldn't be mooning over Ivy.

"Ever since grade school, you assumed you'd marry Cami. Thus, Ivy's just your rebound chick." Wynton sipped his drink.

"She's more than a rebound." He liked hanging out with Ivy, making her laugh, even doing mundane things like shopping or watching a movie.

"Maybe so, but she's a human. That adds a huge layer of complications."

"Don't I know it. Relationships are forbidden. Now I understand why. The connection is awesome."

"You slept with her." Wynton raised a brow.

Zander nodded.

"That's serious. I wouldn't tell anyone else if I were you."

"Didn't plan to." The last thing he needed would be to embarrass his family or to be called before the council. "I figured I had everything figured out when I got back to town, but I keep missing her."

"Did you dump her right after you had sex?"

"Not right away. I did break up with her before I came

home. It seemed like the right thing to do." The guilt still gnawed at his gut.

"Sounds smart. How'd you meet her?"

"I met her right after I met with my lawyer."

"Lawyer?"

"I got drunk and was thrown in jail. It's a long story. I'll tell you about it later."

"You'd better." Wynton finished his drink. "Refill?"

"Yes."

"When did you last see her?" Wynton prodded.

"A few hours ago, I visited Ivy and told her I'd like to keep seeing her whenever I was in town. I planned to be there at least every other week." He recalled the ire flashing in her eyes, although he couldn't figure out why.

"So you asked her to be your booty call?" Wynton gave him a no-you-didn't look.

"That's not at all what I meant."

"But that's how it sounded.

"Holy Hades. I blew it with her. How am I going to fix it?"

"Groveling works. Except in your case, you need to decide what you really want. Are you willing to give up everything to be with her?"

"Describe everything." A sinking feeling hit him.

"Your archery job. Your elite status. Your life as you know it in Cupid's Corner."

He hadn't missed any of those things when he was with her but giving them up was too much. Zander put his head in his hands. "I don't know what to do."

"You have to follow your heart. Decide how much she means to you. Do you love her?"

"I'm not sure. Maybe." That question threw him for a loop. He liked her a lot but was it love?

"When do you work next?"

"Tuesday." Work had been the last thing on his mind.

"That gives you three days to figure out what you want. You're welcome to stay here."

"Thanks." Zander motioned for another refill. His tired brain needed a pick me up.

MONDAY AFTERNOON, Zander decided he'd give Rick a visit and try to get him on his side. He could've used the key he still had when he rented a room but knocking on the apartment door seemed better.

He waited, rocking back and forth on his DC skate shoes. Begging had been tough enough, but groveling would take courage. And he'd need a truckload of fortitude to win back Ivy.

"Zander, what are you doing here?" Rick's tone sounded wary.

"Hoping you'll help me win back Ivy."

"Why should I? You broke up with her." Rick glared at him like Ivy's friends had at the restaurant Friday night. "And you didn't even have the nerve to tell me the truth when I took you to the airport."

"I'm sorry. Really." Apologizing had never been his strong suit, but he had to get Ivy back. Plus, he did feel bad he'd lied.

Rick folded his arms.

"That wasn't one of my better moments. Could I come in?" he asked. "Please."

Rick didn't budge.

"Please." A word Zander rarely used. "I need your help."

"Fine." He pulled open the door and motioned for Zander to enter. "It would've been nice if you returned my text."

"Sorry," he cringed as he sat in a chair. That was one word he hated to say, yet lately, he'd used that word several times.

"I assumed I did the right thing for Ivy when I broke up with her. I mean, my family needed my help. I kept busy for the first few weeks and tried to ignore any feelings I had for her. One day at the lake, a woman with long dark hair went by on a sailboat, reminding me how much I missed her."

"She's not only furious at you but hurt."

"She probably hates me."

"Probably. Ivy doesn't open up easily and rarely dates. I should know. I've asked her out enough times. Now I realize she did me a favor. Pen's more my style." Rick cracked his knuckles.

"What can I do to fix things with Ivy?"

"Doubt you can. From what Pen said, you asked Ivy to be your hookup whenever you're in town. That's pretty bad."

"I told her I'd like to see her whenever I came here." The pit of his gut clenched.

"Sounds like the same thing to me."

Wynton had called it a booty call. “It’s not like that,” Zander groaned. “I’m not seeing anyone else.”

“You planning to make Moosehead your permanent home.”

“It’s complicated.” His job allowed him plenty of freedom between assignments, but he couldn’t move here.

“Which is a copout. Until you figure things out, I suggest you leave Ivy alone. Penelope and Sammy have been picking up the pieces. Frankly, my relationship has even suffered a little. If you’re not serious, you might as well go.”

“I am serious. I can’t live without her.” A dull ache thumped in his heart. He had thought long and hard about his dilemma. The easiest thing for him would be to continue being a Cupid archer. That’s what his family and even the community expected from him. He didn’t plan to leave them behind like Cami had done to him. He and Ivy could still be together when he wasn’t on assignment. If he got a chance to speak with her, he would explain. Ivy would understand—he hoped.

“I get it, but I doubt Ivy will.”

Zander needed a grand gesture to win her back. An idea popped into his head. He checked the clock. Half-past four. The florist should still be open.

CHAPTER 32

Friday at work, Ivy received a bouquet of pink peonies with a card that read: *I'm sorry.*

She threw the flowers in the trash. Who did he think he was? She refused to be anyone's mistress. Something in her head told her to google him.

Why hadn't she thought to do this before?

Alexander Eros, Heavenly Valley.

Several names came up on Facebook. None of the photos were him. The same thing for Instagram. In the white pages, she found an Alex Eros in Oakland.

Usually, she didn't use the work computer for personal issues. But today, she didn't care. She found his address listed, googled it, and zoomed in on an older apartment building close to the slopes.

Okay. This looked like somewhere he might live. She quickly closed the map, feeling like a stalker.

His last employer was listed as Cupid Bows and Arrows. She did a search. Owned by the Sterling Corporation, it had been in the Sterling family since 1960—not the Eros family.

What a liar.

She picked up the phone and called Sammy. "I'm an idiot."

"That's nonsense. You're one of the smartest people I know." Sammy's sing-song tone didn't calm Ivy because she was pissed. "What happened?"

"Zander had the nerve to send me flowers."

"It could be worse."

"Not really. Flowers. Isn't that what a man might send to his mistress. I refuse to play that game."

"With good reason."

Once she had finished talking about Zander, she could breathe a little easier.

SATURDAY, carnations were left on her doorstep.

Please forgive me.

She dropped the gift into the dumpster.

A knock came at her condo on Sunday, miniature roses.

I made a big mistake.

She crumbled the note and set the flowers on her neighbor's doorstep.

Monday Gladys handed her azaleas.

I miss you.

Tuesday, petunias.

I miss your smile.

Wednesday, hibiscuses.

I miss us.

Thursday, he sent a dozen long stem red roses.

I'll be waiting for you at the entrance of

Moosehead State Park tomorrow night.

7 p.m.

I'm miserable without you. Please come.

Z

How dare he? If Zander thought flowers would get her to take him back, he was certifiable. Even if she wasn't boarding a plane for Rhapsody Island tomorrow morning, she wouldn't go to him.

Gladys brought in a paper for Ivy to sign. "Red Roses. Somebody thinks you're special."

"Take them, please. They're getting in my way."

"They smell good." Gladys leaned down and sniffed a flower. "I could press them for you and make a potpourri for your dresser drawer."

"That's okay." She had no intention of ever letting Zander back in her life.

"Do you have everything for your trip?"

“I’m packed and more than ready to go.” Ivy hoped a change of scenery would take her out of her perpetual funk.

“Be sure to enjoy that lovely grandmother of yours. She is such a sweetie.”

“That she is.” Ivy’s grandmother occasionally called her at the office and chatted with Gladys. Happiness bubbled inside her. In less than twenty-four hours, she would be in paradise and far away from thoughts of Zander.

Friday night

Zander thought he’d been pretty clever last week setting up the floral deliveries before he headed back to Cupid’s Corner. His gesture had been significant. She must have forgiven him by now, right?

Today, after finishing an assignment in Utah, he arrived at the top of Caribou Cove around six. Except for a couple of fishermen in a rowboat, the place appeared empty. Still, in Cupid form, he used magic to create a checkerboard blanket and spread it on the ground. More than a month ago, Ivy sat next to him on a similar blanket, and they’d shared their first kiss,

She’d come.

After all, he was Alexander Eros. The best archer in Cupid’s Corner. The Golden Boy.

His bravado suddenly wavered. Once he showed her his true self, she would realize why he couldn’t be there all the time. He just couldn't give up his life, but he would spend every free minute with her. They had to make their relationship work. A part of him wished he were human and could live in Moosehead full-time and woo her back into his arms. Too bad things had to be so convoluted.

Flicking his fingertips, he created a bottle of champagne on ice, a picnic basket filled with cheese, crackers, strawberries dipped in chocolate, and a single red rose. He programmed his phone with old love songs.

Swirling dust around his body, he transformed into a tuxedo and glanced down. Too fancy. He used his dust one more time and changed into a sky-blue polo shirt and gray cargo pants.

He checked the time on his phone. Six-thirty-three. With a rose in his hand, he walked to the park's front entrance to meet Ivy's bus.

The manager greeted him. "Hey, Zander. You interested in a cabin for the weekend. Someone just canceled."

Fate must be rooting for him. "I'll take it." He pulled out a hundred-dollar bill, handed it to the man, headed for the trolley stop near the street, and waited at a bench.

Six-fifty-two. Ivy should be here soon. Butterflies filled his stomach.

The trolley came to a stop. A couple with kids got off. "You getting on?" the driver asked.

"No." He tried not to be disappointed. Ivy would be on the next trolley. The door hissed closed. In the distance, a coyote called his mate. He checked his phone for messages. Nothing.

The next trolley rambled past without even slowing.

Okay. Maybe fate wasn't on his side. He checked the time. Seven-fifteen. No reason to panic. An owl hooted. Crickets chirped. Traffic wooshed by.

Another trolley stopped. A group with Camp Moosehead T-shirts straggled off. The final person was a dark-haired woman. Zander's heart sped up until she got closer, and he saw the face wasn't her. Cursed Cyclops.

Zander checked his phone. Seven-forty-eight. "Is this the last trolley from town?"

"Yes, sir. I'm heading back to turn the trolley into the station."

"Is it okay if I get on?" He would knock on Ivy's door and, if necessary, force her to talk with him.

"Sure."

He took a seat near the front and sent her a text.

Are you coming?

He watched his phone.

Message failed to send.

It wouldn't surprise him if she blocked his number.

Now he was angry. With plenty of sunlight left, he got off at the next stop and took the closest sunbeam up to Cupid's Corner.

Minutes later, he paced inside his apartment.

His doorbell chimed. Now what? He parted the cloud-covered doorway. "Uncle Andre." If his uncle got wind of the offenses Zander committed on Earth, his goose would be cooked so to speak. "What can I do for you?"

"I was in the area and figured I'd stop by. We rarely get to chat." Living on the family's estate, his uncle often acted as his mentor. In fact, his uncle taught him how to shoot his first arrow and encouraged Zander to enter his first contest at age four. Which he won.

"Come on in. Let's share an ambrosia."

"I'd like that." They entered the kitchen, and his uncle sat at a bar stool. Zander flicked his fingertips. Dust swirled with fluted glasses of pink liquid.

His uncle sipped his drink. "How are you, really? I mean, it must be hard considering you've loved Cami for most of your life."

Zander thought he loved her. "I'll admit I *had* been pretty upset, but I'm fine now."

"Glad to hear that." Uncle Andre smiled. "You can't fight destiny. One day, the right woman will come along and capture your heart."

"I'm in no hurry to fall in love." An image of Ivy came to mind, and he pushed it away.

"Well, I just wanted to make sure you're all right." He finished his drink. "Remember, I'm here for you."

"Thanks, Uncle Andre. You're the best." He walked him to the door. Uncle Andre made some excellent points. Chasing after Ivy made no sense. One day he'd find his true love.

CHAPTER 33

Late Saturday afternoon, after two transfers and ten hours to Nassau, Ivy rode in the front of a four-seater puddle-jumper.

"You must be Heliconia's granddaughter," the pilot said as a young couple sat behind her and spoke to each other.

"I am." Jetlag hit her, and she yawned.

"She's excited you're coming."

"I am elated to be here." A sailboat drifting along the turquoise blue ocean similar to the one she took with her five-year-old brother, Jed, when she held him on her lap. At eight, she'd been responsible for him. They arrived safely, but it had been an enormous stress for her at such a young age.

"We're about to land," the pilot said.

Fishing boats lined the north side. Lush plants and palm

trees covered the interior, along with huts and houses. Past the sandy beaches, surfers bobbed in the waves. The plane skidded in the water along the east shoreline.

Once she stepped off the plane and onto the beach, she took off her shoes. Her steps light as smooth, soft, ultrafine sand squeezed between her toes. Warmth radiated throughout her heart as she rushed toward Grammy.

"You're here." Her grandmother placed a lei around her neck. Her face had a few more wrinkles, and a tinge of gray showed in her dark hair, but she still wore the same endearing smile.

"I've missed you." Ivy breathed in the sweet scent of the lei's hibiscuses and hugged this beloved woman.

"As have I." Grammy let her go and eyed her. "You're far too thin. I've got key lime pie waiting for you at my hut."

Ivy made key lime for Zander. What an idiot she'd been to believe his lies. Her stomach twisted. At least she never showed for the date at the state park. Hopefully, he waited all night.

She and Grammy walked along the dirt path side by side, breathing in the salty scent of the ocean. The humidity moistened her skin as the breeze cooled her face. What a special place.

They passed three huts and came to Grammy's. Adobe walls. Thatched roof. Wicker chairs on the porch with hand-sewn cushions. A chair swing hung under the eaves to the far left.

She advanced up the three steps and held the door for her

grandmother. She could count on both hands the number of times she had visited Grammy's house, yet nostalgia hit her as she glanced around the room. Grammy's comfortable chair remained in the corner next to the reading lamp with a beaded lampshade. The open room leading to the kitchen still smelled like plumeria and cinnamon. Shelves held canned foods and jars of fruits and jams. Pots and pans hung on a bamboo rack above the old stove. This place felt like comfort.

"Mind setting the table?"

"Not at all." Ivy pulled out two bright orange ceramic plates from the cupboard and found the silverware in the drawer to the side of the sink. When she grabbed the glasses, a memory of being a little girl drinking pineapple juice with her Grammy and Gramps hit her. Happy times of being loved.

Grammy placed a dish of rice with skewers of fish, pineapple and mangoes in front of her.

Ivy took a bite. "This is delicious. I forgot how fresh everything tastes on the island."

"What are your plans while you're here?"

"I'd like to go surfing tomorrow."

"You and your brother were little when you came, but you both took to the water like porpoises." Grammy shook her head.

"Gramps was patient. I miss him." Ivy recalled the dark-haired man with the non-stop smile. "That summer will always be one of my all-time favorites."

"You should have heard him laugh when he told me how many times you fell off your board into the water. He loved you." Grammy had a far-off look. Gramps had been gone ten years, and Ivy could tell Grammy still missed him. "I tried to talk Jed into coming with me, but he's busy with work."

"He will come when it's his time. Right now, you're the one who needs healing."

And she wasn't wrong. Ivy had to get over Zander once and for all. Her grandmother's uncanny intuition must've kicked in. Ivy recalled visiting here as a teen. Grammy had been busy, so she went to the beach and got stung by a jellyfish. The pain had been unbearable as she stumbled out of the water. Grammy appeared, brought her to a blanket on the shore, poured vinegar on the wound, and used tweezers to remove the stinger.

Over the years, Grammy seemed to sense when Ivy needed her most. She would call at the right moment to soothe Ivy's frustration about moving to a different town or when she worried about finals or just needed a pep talk. Whenever life got topsy-turvy, Grammy remained her pillar of strength.

"Are you ready to talk about Zander?"

Ivy wished she had never brought him up, wished she hadn't confided in Grammy during their frequent phone calls. "No need. I'm over him."

"Then you are not being honest with yourself."

"What do you expect me to do, act as his mistress whenever he chooses to be in town?" Ivy refused to be at anyone's beck and call. "He doesn't respect me."

"Yet you still love him."

"No, I don't." Tired of dredging up their time together, she'd washed her hands of him. "I'm a realist. Love doesn't last."

"Someday, you will be ready to accept your destiny. Someday, the right man will show you genuine love."

Ivy picked up both plates and rinsed the utensils off in the sink. "The kind of love you and Gramps shared no longer exists."

"I am afraid your mother's continual attempt to replace your father has tarnished your ability to believe in love."

"Enough about my love life. Can we talk about something else?" The discussion had Ivy's stomach knotting up.

"Are you ready to venture into the enchanted rainforest?"

"Not that fable nonsense again." Ivy counted silently in her head to ten. Grammy had said her father came from a prestigious line of pixies and faeries.

"You're rose birthmark sparkles with light pink. It's a sign." When Grammy got something in her head, she had a hard time letting it go. "Let's sit on the veranda and enjoy the beautiful evening.

"Sure." Ivy held the door for Grammy, and they sat in wicker chairs.

"I know you don't care to talk about your heritage, but it's time you embraced the magic."

"Magic doesn't exist."

"That's because you don't believe," Grammy placed a hand over her heart. "Do you remember living on this island with both your parents?"

"Not really. Dad died shortly after I turned two."

"Your father had magical powers, but they couldn't protect him from the boating accident that took his life." Grammy frowned.

"What if I pretend what you say is true? Tell me why my father didn't use his magic to blink himself out of the situation?" She seriously doubted Grammy would have an answer.

"Gramps told me that an unexpected mast fell, hit him and knocked him unconscious. A wave washed on the deck, swept your father into the water, and he drowned."

"Did they ever find his body?" Ivy had to ask.

"Yes." Grammy did a cross over her chest. "Your mother had been inconsolable. She blamed herself because she had an argument with him before he left. In her grief-stricken state, she couldn't stay on Rhapsody."

"Whenever I bring up dad, mom gets upset. It's easier to say nothing."

"Even after all of these years, his death is still hard for her to talk about." Grammy's eyes misted. "She was angry that his magic did nothing to save him and thought you'd be better off if you never used it. That's why she made me promise not to mention your powers until you were older, and I honored her."

"You sure love telling strange tales." A part of Ivy wanted

to believe what Grammy said was real, but she struggled to buy into the craziness.

"When I first mentioned the truth, you assumed I lost my mind." Grammy patted her hand.

"It does sound pretty ridiculous." Ivy stared into Grammy's lucid eyes. If only what she said were true.

"Your magical abilities can be restored when you enter the cavern. From what I've been told, the waterfall in the enchanted land can fully replenish your abilities. It's your heritage, one you should embrace to honor your father."

"If my father was a fae, show me a photo of him with wings?" What would her life be like if he had lived?

"I never took any." Her eyes softened. "You have his rich brown eyes and wide smile."

Ivy wiped away the tear dripping down her cheek with her fingertips. She needed to be alone with her thoughts. Why was she fearful to journey into the enchanted rainforest? "Jet lag's hitting me, and I'm going to lie down." She kissed Grammy's cheek.

"Tomorrow, we'll talk more. There is still much to discuss." Grammy enveloped her in a hug.

CHAPTER 34

Ivy dreamed she hiked on a steep embankment and slipped off the trail. "Reach for my fingers," Zander called and held out his hand, but she couldn't quite grasp it.

Falling, falling, falling.

She abruptly opened her eyes to see yellow eyes that reflected like a beacon. "Hey, Taffy." Her grandmother's cat mewed and ran out the door.

Ivy fluffed her pillow and settled under the covers.

What a dream! The infamous anxiety-induced falling dream. She hadn't had that dream in at least four years. It must've been about her first day of college. Anxiety wasn't precisely her problem now. Frustration, worry, and disbelief better described her situation.

Sunlight filtered in through the top of the window. She might as well get up.

Grammy sipped tea at the kitchen table. “Morning.”

She grabbed a cup of coffee, sipped the rich brew, and couldn’t help smiling. “You made mochi waffles?”

“Of course. I picked mangos and bananas and kiwi yesterday, so they’re fresh.”

“You’re a saint.” She topped her food with fruit and took a bite. Yum. The sweet bread made with rice flour practically sang on her tongue. Memories of being little and helping Grammy mix the batter flooded her mind. “This is delicious. I’ve always loved your cooking.”

“So did your father. Your mother never cared much for being in the kitchen, but she got better over time.”

“Not much. We ate a lot of peanut butter and jelly sandwiches growing up.” To this day, Ivy couldn’t stand anything with peanut butter in it.

“What was mom like when she met dad?”

“Happy. She smiled all the time. Loved to laugh. Loved to surf.” Grammy added more fruit to her waffle.

“You’ve said that before. I can’t imagine mom surfing.” She couldn’t recall ever seeing her mom swimming much less riding a wave.

“That girl could be fearless in the water. I believe her bravado is what drew your father to her.” Grammy’s eyes lit.

“Don’t you have a photo of her with her board?” Ivy had finished her meal and rinsed her plate in the sink.

“I do. Let’s sit in the living room and look through my album.”

They moved to the couch. Grammy pulled out a hand-made photo album bound together with leather ties and flipped through the pages. She stopped on a photo of a skinny teenager in an orange and pink bikini.

"How old was she?

"Sixteen or seventeen. The next summer she met your dad." Grammy turned to the next page. "Married right after she graduated. They were young, but Gramps and I knew they belonged together."

She stared at her father's picture seeing her own eyes in his.

"You said he had magical powers."

"He did." Grammy tilted her head. "Are you finally starting to believe what I've told you?"

"It's pretty farfetched." She needed proof. "How did you know my dad was a fae?"

"I had sensed his abilities and talked with him about it. Your mother knew the truth before she married him. Before he asked Gramps for her hand, he transformed into a ruler-sized person with light blue wings. I happened to be in the room."

"And you weren't in shock? I would have been." As far as Ivy was concerned, magic didn't exist. Except something in the back of her mind remained curious.

"This is Rhapsody. I've befriended many faes over the years. The only thing they ask of me is to not share their secret with anyone."

"Why haven't I ever seen any?" None of this made sense.

"Because faeries usually visit me in human form, but

occasionally I've had tea inside the house with a couple of them. I find their tiny bodies fascinating. My tales about the little people with wings were from seeing them firsthand. This island has special powers that give the fae the ability to transform into human shape. You have to believe in the impossible." She put her hand over Ivy's.

"I don't get it. If I possess magic, shouldn't I be able to feel the power?" At the thought, a tingling spark seemed to arc through Ivy.

"According to my fae friends, the vortex supposedly charges a fae's power, but if they leave Rhapsody their magical powers dissipate quickly."

"You've talked with others about me?"

"Of course." Grammy smirked. "How else could I learn how to help you?"

"Do all half-human faes have magical abilities?" In this strange world Grammy had concocted, it almost made sense that genetics might factor into things.

"There's a 50/50 chance that hybrids receive the gift. Your ankle rose birthmark comes from your father's clan. Since you left the island two weeks after your rose appeared, you never had a chance to fully develop your powers." Grammy patted her hand.

Ivy looked at her rose. It now glimmered silvery pink.

CHAPTER 35

All week long, Zander's concentration had been off. Typically, he looked forward to his assignments. He had been proud of his superb marksmanship that allowed him to assist relationships with his love potion arrows. However, lately, anytime he shot a love arrow, he got aggravated with Ivy. His romantic gestures should have swept her off her feet. She should have shown up for the dinner he'd planned. He would have swayed her to see that they belonged together.

As the Minnow Lake Lodge in South Dakota came into view, the wooded area reminded him of Moosehead. He landed on top of an oak mantle with ease and searched for his assignment. Two people behind the concierge counter were engrossed in a conversation and didn't look in his direction.

Baked goods mixed with the scent of pine. People sat on couches and chairs. Across the shiny wooden floors, customers sat on barstools drinking assorted beverages. An amber-colored aura flickered from the couple nearest the end.

"If you loved me ..." a man's voice said softly, "you'd understand why I have to go."

Bingo. He'd found the couple.

Now to recall the couple's file. He tapped his heart emblem on his wrist, pulled up a screen, and skimmed the info. The man took a job in Seattle and didn't ask her to come.

Their love lights faded. A love boost would restore what the man really desired—for her to be with him.

Time to complete his task. He took his quiver and bow off his shoulder, snatched an arrow, nocked it in place, and floated lower.

The man stood facing his girlfriend with her hands on her hips. Perfect angle. He flew in a few feet closer and released his arrow. Zing. Dark pink lit the heart.

"I can't ask you to move away from your family or the job you love," the boyfriend said.

"I love you. I'll be happy to be wherever you are?" The man pulled her into his arms, kissing her passionately.

Success. The scene touched him. His own happiness came from being around Ivy.

Wynton's words kept haunting him. *"Do you love her?"*

What he had with Ivy was special and well-worth upping the ante. Now to figure out how to see her. Fate must've put them together, and he could use fate to help him. He closed his eyes.

Rhapsody echoed in his mind.

"Rhapsody," he said out loud and racked his brain for the meaning. Rhapsody Island. Ivy's grandmother. No wonder his message never sent. Ivy left the country for her vacation.

He had to go to her. Still, in his Cupid form, he fluttered outside the lodge and tapped his heart-shaped wrist emblem. "How to get to Rhapsody from here?" he asked.

A virtual map popped up and highlighted one of the islands outside of the Bahamas. He'd been to Cuba which appeared to be about two hundred miles closer, and knew which sunbeam in the Calypso Forest would bring him there.

His emblem flashed 2:56. That gave him plenty of time to grab a few things from his apartment and create extra vials of magical dust. He caught the closest ray of light and ascended to Cupid's Corner.

Several minutes later, he arrived at his place, parted the cloud-covered door, headed for his closet, and sifted through a container for a small red velvet box. He flicked his fingertips and created several glass vials, flicked again to add his dust, tucking the bottles and a box in a side pocket in his backpack. He added some snacks, swim trunks, shorts and two T-shirts, and headed out ready to pursue Ivy.

Traveling east along the Fates River until it hit the border of Dione's Cove, he found the sunbeam in front of three maple trees. He zoomed down the sunbeam and landed on top of a gift shop in the Bahamas.

"Last call for Eureka, Finnigan, and Rhapsody," a skipper called from an island hopper boat with bench seats along the back.

This worked because he didn't care to fight the strong tailwind he'd face flying across this section of the Atlantic Ocean.

An older man and woman stepped aboard. Zander fluttered over them toward the hardtop above the helm and cockpit and perched himself along the back edge and dangled his legs. As a Cupid, few humans would notice him.

"Hello," an elfin faery whispered as she floated next to him with sparkly amethyst wings and a matching short gown. She flipped her ebony-colored ponytail and eased into a spot inches from where he sat. "Are you new around here?" She batted her long lashes.

"Name's Zander."

"Veronica." She shook his hand.

"I'm going to Rhapsody."

"What a coincidence. I live on that island." She smiled, her dark eyes holding his. "I'd be more than happy to show you around."

"Not this time. I'm visiting a friend." The boat took off, and he gripped the top with his fingers.

"Who?"

"Ivelisse Venturi."

"Venturi sounds familiar, but I don't think she lives in the enchanted rainforest."

"She's visiting her grandmother." The boat slowed along the shore. "Are there many faeries living in the forest?"

"Over two hundred. Many live double lives acting as humans for most of the time and visiting the waterfall to replenish their magic." Her ponytail bobbed as they hit a wave. "Our enchanted rainforest is one of the few places in the world fae like to live."

"Interesting." No wonder the name sounded familiar. The island had a magical realm. He had brought six vials of dust to ensure his ability to transform but may not need them.

"What's the grandmother's name?"

He thought for a second. "It might be Carol or Connie."

"If it's Connie, I know her. She's a nice lady, and her key lime pie is to die for."

Ivy had used her grandmother's recipe.

"It was nice meeting you, Zander. Enjoy the island atmosphere." Veronica smiled brightly as the boat docked. "If things don't work out with your lassie, give me a call. She flicked purple dust from her fingertips and created a sparkly calling card that floated into his hand."

"Could you point me in the direction of Connie's place?"

"Go north along the east path and make a right at Paradise Avenue. It's the fourth hut on the left. Good luck.

Aloha." Veronica flew off the boat, turned back his way and waved. Cute, but she wasn't Ivy.

Now to change into human form. He flew off the top, ducked behind a coconut tree, and swirled his dust around him. In seconds, he transformed into a mortal wearing swim trunks, a Hawaiian shirt, flip-flop shoes while holding his full-sized backpack. Walking the few short blocks, he arrived at the hut. His stomach clenched as he approached the door and knocked.

A striking woman walked out the front door. "May I help you?"

"Hello." He flashed her a smile. "I'd like to speak with Ivy."

The woman eyed him from top to bottom and frowned. "I sense you are the man who broke my granddaughter's heart."

"I didn't do it intentionally." He swallowed hard. "Hurting Ivy had never been my purpose."

"Nonetheless, you did, Mr.?"

"Zander Eros."

"Eros … hmmm … are you related to the Cupid, Andrew Eros?" Her dark eyes softened. "If so, you have his sky-blue eyes."

"He's my great grandfather. Wait. Did you just call my grandfather a Cupid?" Cupids are rarely seen in their natural form.

"I did. About six decades ago. I was just a child when I heard my parents arguing on the front porch. I looked out the window and spotted Andrew nocking his arrow and hitting my father."

His jaw dropped, and he stared at her for several seconds. "Most humans can't see us."

"Being young, my mind was open to the unimaginable. Your grandfather fluttered in the window and whispered in my ear, 'It's all right, little one. My arrow should help your mom and dad stop fighting.' Grammy smiled, making her seem much younger. "And I believed him."

"How did you know his name?" He rubbed his eyes.

"He told me. I never saw him again, but after my experience, I visited the edge of the enchanted rainforest and spotted my first faery."

He rocked back and forth on his heels.

"Are you aware that the ruby heart on your wrist is twinkling?"

He ran his finger over the spot. In Moosehead, the magic in his emblem had dissipated while in jail. "I suppose it is."

"What makes you think you can mend your relationship with my granddaughter?"

"To be honest, I don't know if I can. But I'm here."

"Do you love her?" She raised a brow.

"I do. Without Ivy, I am miserable."

Her grandmother folded her arms. "Is she aware that you're a Cupid?"

"Not yet, but I plan to show her today. If she'll see me, I'll be honest with her about everything. I'll do whatever it takes to be with her." He shuddered. This woman could shoot him down, and then what would he do? "Will you help me try to win Ivy back, please?"

She shook her head. "That will be up to Ivy; however, I do wish you luck."

"But I don't have your blessing."

"Again, my granddaughter must make up her own mind. And you must show her your true self."

"I will. Would you at least tell me where to find her?"

"She's at the northwest end surfing."

"Ivy mentioned learning with her brother. I've never tried. Maybe she'll teach me—that is if she ever forgives me."

"It won't be easy getting her to forgive you. Ivy can be a bit hardheaded at times." Her grandmother chuckled. "Anyway, take the trail to the west until it hits the cliffs. Follow the stone steps down to the beach. You can't miss it."

"Thanks." He hugged the woman that meant the world to Ivy.

Still in human form, he walked along the dirt path and sensed vibrations flowing through his body similar to a mild electric charge. This must be the effects of the enchanted vortex.

A parrot landed on the branch of a palm tree. "Stay the course," it squawked. "Stay the course." The parrot opened its wings. "Stay the course," it called once more and fluttered off. Weird. More than weird.

He continued on the trail to the stone steps and marveled at the view of the pristine turquoise ocean and about a dozen black suits bobbing on boards. He kept going to the sandy beach. A wave broke, and his focus riveted on the surfer. He recognized Ivy's lithe body as she moved with the board. Her motions were fluid and free as she rode inside the barrel of the wave to the shore. Standing, she held her board under her arm and headed in his direction.

"Hey, Ivy," he called.

CHAPTER 36

With her hand above her eyes, Ivy squinted. “Zander. What are you doing here?” He’d just invaded her private life, making her livid.

He stepped closer and rubbed his stubbled jaw. “I came to see you.”

“I told you I never wanted to see you again.” Her scowl said volumes.

“I can’t live without you in my life.”

“For how long? A week? Maybe a month?” Men couldn’t be trusted for the long haul—especially him.

“Longer if you’ll let me. Please. We need to talk, somewhere private.”

She set her board in the sand, dried off with her towel, and put on a coverup dress. “No, thanks.”

He glanced around the area. The closest people were about six yards away. "Please."

"Nope." She put on her flip-flops, grabbed her board, and hurried toward the stairs.

He followed behind her up the stone steps. "We had something good until I left. I should have been honest from the start."

"Yes, you should have." She practically stomped to the top.

"But I'm here now. That should count for something."

She gave a sardonic laugh and kept walking.

"I need to tell you about my life." Which he found hard considering he had to tell her about his true self.

"Yeah, like how your family doesn't own a bow and arrow factory. I despise liars." She let out a long sigh. "Leave me alone."

"I had reasons for what I did."

"And I'm supposed to accept your sorry excuses and forgive you?" She huffed.

"Yes." Damn, she was angry, and he couldn't blame her. In her mind, he wanted to use her.

"Go away. Let me enjoy my vacation."

"I'm not going anywhere until you hear me out." He motioned toward a relatively secluded bench several yards away behind a tree.

"Dammit, Zander." Her eyes flared with fire.

"Ten minutes. Then I'll leave you alone. I promise." Begging was hard, but he had to get her to listen.

"Five." She set her board against the tree and remained standing.

He stood next to her. "First off, I never meant to hurt you."

"Right." She folded her arms.

"I certainly never expected to fall for you."

Her lips curled, and she bared her teeth.

This wasn't going well.

"I grew up in an affluent family in Cupid's Corner." His right eye twitched, and he hoped she didn't notice.

"Where's that?"

"Up in the heavenly realm." He pointed to the clouds above them.

"That's it." She took a step, but he stopped her with his arm. "You promised me five minutes."

Her lips flattened, and fire flashed in her eyes, making it hard to think.

He had to get through to her. "Before arriving in Moosehead, I had been drinking to try and ease the pain because my ex just got married. It wasn't enough to be drunk, but I had a pretty good buzz."

"And you went to a bar and got arrested?"

"Not exactly. What I'm about to tell you will sound crazy, but please try and listen with an open mind."

She glanced at her phone. "You're down to four minutes."

"Well … while I indulged in self-pity, I got a reminder of an assignment … and headed down a sunbeam to shoot a love potion arrow to fix a troubled couple."

She squinted at him like he were crazy. "That's the lamest excused I've ever heard."

"You've seen me shoot. What I didn't tell you is I'm a Cupid archer. I shoot arrows of love into people."

"This is ridiculous." She tapped her foot. He could tell she had lost her patience with him.

A group of surfers walked past. "I can prove it, but we need to go somewhere more private."

"No thanks."

Once the surfers were no longer in view, he flicked his fingertips, swirled his magical dust, and produced a red rose. "For you." He handed the flower to her.

Her eyes widened. "Did you just create a rose?"

"My magical dust did." He had her attention.

"This is impossible." She twirled the rose.

"Child's play. I can shapeshift."

"Shapeshift?" She stared at him like he belonged in an asylum.

"As I told you, I'm a Cupid. Are you up to seeing me transform?" He didn't wish to scare her in his real shape, but he had to get her to see reason.

"Show me."

"Are you sure? I'm going to shrink to be fourteen and a half inches."

"I can handle it." Her lips pressed together.

He flicked his fingertips and a ruby-colored cloud surrounded him. His body shrank, and he fluttered above her, wearing a sparkling red suit.

"This can't be happening." Except for her rapid blinking, she remained frozen.

"Please don't freak, Ivy." He swirled his dust, turned into his human shape, sat next to her, and reached for her hand.

She pushed him away. "What do you expect me to do? You're a Cupid."

"I'm still me. I'm still your friend and lover."

She shook her head. "You're nothing but a fraud."

"What we had was real. Is real." His eyes got misty, something they never did. He couldn't lose Ivy.

"I can't do this." She stood.

"I get it. You need time to process everything and talk to your grandmother." He grabbed her board.

"I can carry that."

"Indulge me. I came all this way to see you. Let me walk you home."

"Fine." Her voice came out small and defeated.

They walked along the path side by side without saying a word, turned up her grandmother's street, and stopped outside her hut.

"I'll swing by tomorrow morning." He moved forward inches from her and searched her eyes, but the frown that marred her face had him back up a few steps. He had to take things slow. "Meet me on the porch if you'd like to see me."

She said nothing.

He longed to pull her in his arms or at the very least kiss her on the cheek but figured the shock of seeing him as a

Cupid had her in a confused state. But he could be patient with her. He had to win her back.

His chest tightened. What if she never accepted him?

Ivy walked into the hut and found her grandmother sitting in a rocking chair. "Did that young man find you?"

"Yes. Grammy, I'm more confused than ever." She plunked onto the couch.

"Because he's a Cupid."

"How did you know?" Grammy had talked about pixies and faeries but never Cupids.

"I saw his great grandfather shoot a love arrow. It fixed my parent's marriage." Her grandmother was full of surprises.

"You met his grandfather?"

"Once as a little girl. I've been told by my fae friends that most people can't see supernaturals." Grammy winked at her.

"Have I met any of those friends?" She would have remembered

"Possibly, but probably when they used glamour to hide their identity and appear human."

Could things get any stranger? "My father is fae, but I never truly believed you."

"And you do now?"

"Zander turned into a Cupid. He had freaking wings." Ivy still couldn't understand it.

"Seeing a supernatural can be upsetting at first, but you eventually get used to it." Her eyes softened.

"You think?"

Grammy placed her hand over Ivy's.

"I wish I could remember my dad. After seeing Zander, I'm starting to believe Dad was a fae. Mom said he was the love of her life."

"They were soulmates. She keeps looking for someone to replace your father, but Darren still holds her heart."

That explains her many marriages. "Do you think I have magical powers?"

"Probably. Your glittering rose appeared right before you left the island. Without visiting the enchanted rainforest, you never got to experience your non-human side."

"What do you mean?"

"Once you left the island, your power dissipated."

"I don't get it. How does the rainforest help with magical powers?" All this magical stuff confused her.

"A vortex exists in the enchanted forest underneath the waterfall. My fae friends say the vortex restores all powers within."

"What?"

"I don't entirely get the concept, but I can feel the magnetic power this island possesses. It gives me an inner happiness." Grammy steepled her hands.

"Have you been to the rainforest?"

"On the outskirts. To get into the deep center, you have to go through a cavern that's too small for a human to fit."

"But you tried?"

"Many times." She laughed. "The opening's fairly wide, but it narrows. I watched my faery friend fly up through a hole in the top."

"Couldn't your friend use her magic to make you smaller?" She asked, amazed at how she had started to accept this nonsense as truth. After seeing Zander small and with wings, nothing made sense anymore.

"They have the power of glamour and can conceal themselves, but their innate magic is limited."

Deep in her soul, Ivy knew what Grammy said must be correct. "

"What should I do?"

"Visit the enchanted rainforest and find your way to the waterfall." The corner of Grammy's lips tipped up. "If I were you, I'd ask Zander to bring me."

A part of her rebuked the comment. The other part of her made her heart beat faster.

CHAPTER 37

Zander raked his fingers through his hair. What if Ivy didn't want him?

Never in his life had he worried like he had last night when he'd spent the night on the beach. Never in his life had anyone's opinion mattered as much to him. Unfortunately, he blew everything by showing his true Cupid form. Never in his life had he been so helpless.

He walked along the path that overlooked the ocean and spotted a local woman seated under a palm tree taking flowers from a basket and sewing a beautiful lei. Next to her, she had set out several varieties of flowers.

He reached down to examine one of the leis with pink hibiscus and some other pink flowers. The colors reminded him of selling Ivy those hot pink tennis shoes when he first worked at the skateboard shop. The attraction had been so strong that he asked her out. "I'd like to buy this one." He handed her a twenty. "Keep the change."

"You are most kind." The woman's dark eyes glittered. "May the lei bring you and your love happiness."

"That's what I'm hoping. Aloha." As he strolled away, his steps seemed a bit lighter. The local woman had wished him happiness. Surely that was great luck.

He turned the corner and approached the hut, finding Ivy sitting on a rattan chair swinging her foot back and forth. She'd braided her hair, allowing him to view her pretty face, pert mouth and those expressive chocolate-colored eyes he adored. The eyes that wouldn't meet his. Not a good sign with her.

"Hey." He stepped onto the porch and handed her a lei. "This is for you. It's supposed to bring you happiness."

"Thank you." She set it around her neck and brought one of the flowers under her nose. "The scent of plumeria always reminds me of this island."

"Good to know. That and your favorite color is pink." Hot pink if he were to be specific. He liked her in pink, but today she wore a charcoal black sundress.

"Used to be my favorite." She motioned to the wicker chair next to her. "Have a seat."

"What's wrong?" He'd caused the awkward tension between them. Not that he could have changed leaving her. He made that decision because he had no other choice. His world needed him. The problem was that he didn't know if he'd be happy without Ivy.

"You told me from the start that you'd return home. I just never expected your home would be in another realm." She canted her head. "Seeing you yesterday as a Cupid, well, it's pretty bizarre."

"But I'm still me."

She flipped her braid behind her back. "Not really."

He wished he could read her thoughts. Would she ever accept him for himself? "Because of you, I liked living in Moosehead. Once several weeks had gone by, I found myself content and stopped worrying about getting home. But then I spotted an old friend who gave me a vial of magical dust, and I knew I had to go back. "My archer job is important to my community and to the humans I help."

"That's why you broke up with me?"

"Breaking up with you was the hardest thing I've ever faced. It killed me to see the sparkle in your eyes vanish because of me." He hated the rift he had caused. "I zoomed up a sunbeam."

"What's that like?"

"Fast. I'll have to show you sometime."

"Not gonna happen." She tapped her foot. "What else did you do?"

"I hung out with old friends, went back to work, and attempted to push away what we had but couldn't."

"I can't forgive you. Not after you asked me to be your mistress." She clenched her fists.

He sucked in a deep breath. "I never said that."

"You said you wanted to see me whenever you were in town. Same thing."

"No, it's not. I had figured out a way to see you while continuing with my Cupid assignments. It was the only solution I could come up with." He had to get her to see his side.

"Which is not acceptable for me."

"I'm not sure if I can move to Moosehead permanently."

"I'd never expect you to change your life for me." Her words cut him to the core.

"There has to be another way. Maybe we can figure it out later." They had to make their relationship work.

"I just don't know."

"I never meant to lie to you, but—"

"After seeing you as a Cupid, I'm more confused than ever."

"Don't be." He reached over the armrest of the chair and set his hand on top of hers.

"Grammy says this rose birthmark ties to my father." She crossed her legs, and her ankle rose glittered.

"It's similar to my heart emblem."

"It is." She looked down at the ground. "I've got something more important to figure out."

"You think you might have magical powers?"

She shrugged. "Ever since I was little, Grammy told me stories about my father being a fae. I always assumed they were tall tales."

Ivy might be half faery. Could that be why he had such a strong connection to her?

"If I have powers, why haven't I seen them before?"

"When I am in human form, the magic in my heart emblem dissipates and eventually disappears. That's what happened when I was in Moosehead. I usually bring a couple of vials of magical dust with me so I can transform—except during that trip I forgot."

"For as long as I can remember, my rose birthmark has been a white color." She glanced at her ankle. "Grammy said my powers never fully developed because I left this island as a toddler." She let out a long breath. "She thinks if I visit the enchanted rainforest, I'll be able to tap into my faery side."

"Would you like me to take you?" Hope filled his soul.

"If I am able to shift forms, it'd be helpful to have someone who has done that before."

"I'd be honored." He squeezed her hand. "You'll have to lead the way. I know it's in-between here and the north end."

She stepped down the porch steps, and he followed her along the path.

"I can show you the entrance." She paused for a second. "To be honest, I've never ventured inside."

"Why not? I mean, you're fearless at the skatepark or on the lake." Seagulls cawed overhead as he walked next to her along the path. Palm fronds swayed, creating snatches of mottled shadows. Waves crashed on the sandy shoreline to the west, giving the air a briny scent.

"As a child, I'd heard islanders talk about the mystical properties. Properties that supposedly can change a person into the size of a bird. I didn't like that idea because I wanted to be bigger not smaller."

"You wanted to rule the world." His hand bumped hers and electricity arced where they touched.

"Pretty much."

"If I buy you a diamond tiara, could I be your favorite subject?" Role-playing could definitely spice up their relationship.

"Favorite?" She laughed. "Not likely."

"Ouch." If only she would forgive him.

"I'm just being honest." Her tone sounded weary.

The vegetation got thicker to the east. A toucan made a clattering squawk from a nearby tree and flew off. The air seemed heavier. The trees' limbs twisted and gnarled.

"We're close. I can feel it." She trod onto some mossy rocks and pushed aside large leaves from a rubber plant. "I see the cavern's entrance." She didn't hesitate, didn't shy away from a beetle crawling along with a giant elephant ear leaf, pushed it aside, and entered the squared-off limestone opening.

A vibration emanating from the ground up caused the skin on his arms and legs to tingle. The upflow generated an exhilaration from deep inside him while an invisible magnetic force seemed to spiral around him.

"Do you feel that?" Ivy asked, her face glimmering with excitement.

"That's the vortex's power."

"It's lit its surging through me." Her voice came out

breathy. Light illuminated a sphere-shaped opening near the top about fifty yards away. "My birthmark's turned neon pink."

"Makes sense. Pink is your favorite color. I mean—was." He couldn't resist taking her hand and weaving his fingers through hers.

"There might be another entry to the enchanted rainforest, but I don't see one. From what Grammy told me, it should be on the other side of the cavern."

"We'll probably have to fly through the opening up above. And since we'll be entering a special land, it would be best if you became faery sized." The idea sent a sizzle inside his heart. He couldn't wait to see her pint-sized with wings.

"How would I do that?"

"I flick my fingers."

"Okay." She tried. "Nothing happened."

"Since this is your first time, you might need to prime your fingertips. Try rubbing them along the rose on your ankle and then flick your pointer finger against your thumb." What he said was all speculation, but he hoped it worked.

Hot pink dust surrounded her, and she became an adorable dark-haired pixie in a short sparkly dress. "Wow. I'm tiny, and you're a giant."

He swirled his dust and changed his form. "Better."

"Much." She gazed at him with such wonder. "How do I fly?"

"Squeeze your shoulder blades together and unfurl your wings."

He watched her eyes widen as hot pink wings formed.

"I have freaking wings. Unbelievable." A giggle escaped. "Now what?"

"Flapping will allow you to float upward."

She fluttered and soared to the top of the cave. "Ouch." Her wings quit moving, and she plummeted into his arms.

"I could get used to this." He pushed a strand of hair behind her ear and pressed his lips to her cheek.

"Put me down. You promised we'd explore the rainforest."

"You make an adorable pixie. If exploration is what you desire, I'll be more than happy to oblige. Hold my hand, and we'll fly together."

"I suppose." She folded her hand inside his.

"What will we see?"

"Faeries and possibly gnomes or trolls." Squeezing her hand, he yanked her a little closer.

"And Cupids?"

"Maybe?" Since their relationship wasn't settled yet, he hoped they wouldn't see anyone from his realm. For some reason, the air inside the cave became heavy, making it hard to breathe. They fluttered through the lighted opening and entered the enchanted rainforest and soared above a canopy of trees abundant with various shades of green.

"What a beautiful place!" Ivy squeezed his hand for dear life. "We need to find the waterfall where the vortex's power is supposed to be the strongest."

"I see it to the north." They fluttered for a minute or two

and landed near a lagoon where ripples formed from the distant waterfall. She let go of her grip on his hand. "I can't believe a place like this exists."

"It is pretty spectacular. How are you doing?" Growing up as a Cupid, he'd taken his wings for granted, but for Ivy this had to be a massive shift in her reality.

"I'm feeling all my senses at once." She reached back and ran her fingertips along her wings. "I'm ecstatic and dumbfounded and still a bit shocked. Never in my wildest dreams did I ever picture myself flying, that is, without being inside of an airplane."

"The pink wings fit your badass image." He chuckled.

"You're one to talk. Sparkly blue is rather flashy." She tapped his wing.

"Nothing wrong with flashy." He found himself grinning. Ivy seemed much more at ease. "Do your powers feel more intense now? Mine do."

"A little." She took off her shoes. "I'm going to wade in the water."

"Good idea." He joined her and took her hand. Magnetic energy tingled up his body.

"I feel like an open electric circuit flows through me." She shivered.

He wrapped his arm around her shoulder and tugged her closer. Glancing at his wrist emblem, it glittered a deep ruby color.

"Thanks for sharing this moment with me." She turned to face him and traced her fingers along his jaw.

He reached for her and brushed his lips against hers. "I've missed you."

She backed away, spread her wings, and did a flip in the air. "I'm a faery. Unbelievable." She did a double and a triple flip and landed in the sand along the shore.

He couldn't take his eyes off her as he moved to stand alongside her. With her ever-widening smile, he'd never seen her happier.

"You decided to visit our rainforest." The pixie from the ferry landed in front of them.

Ivy raised a brow.

"Veronica, this is my girlfriend, Ivy." Calling her his girlfriend might be a bold move since nothing had been settled, but saying it felt right.

"Nice to meet you." Veronica held out her hand and shook Ivy's. "You must be the reason Zander visited Rhapsody."

"She is."

"Have you been to our enchanted land before?" Veronica squinted at Ivy.

"Never," Ivy said.

"You picked one of my favorite spots. It's still early. By noon, there will be dozens of faeries and gnomes frolicking underneath the waterfall. The trolls are night creatures and tend to congregate here closer to sundown." Veronica shuddered. "They like to skinny dip. I don't mean to be judgmental, but the warts that cover their backs are gross."

Zander chose not to comment. "Can you recommend a

more secluded place for us to explore?" At the moment, he would rather not share Ivy's company with anyone else.

"If you prefer quiet, I'd choose the top of a coconut tree in the gnarled grove about a mile northeast of here, or you could find a cove above the waterfall. Avoid Rhapsody Peak because folks tend to flock along the ridge."

Zander put his hand above his eyes and could see the peak to the west.

Veronica's ankle rose flashed with violet sparkles. "My friends are here. It was nice meeting you, but I've gotta flutter." She flew toward the waterfall.

"My day keeps getting weirder."

He expected to see her lips pinched together, not see a beaming smile. "And you love every minute." He kissed her cheek. "Where to my lady? The top of a coconut tree or a cove above this waterfall?"

"Neither. I'd rather practice flying." She floated up and fluttered away.

He had to race to catch up, but he wasn't complaining. He got to spend time with her.

CHAPTER 38

Air streamed over her wings as Ivy soared above the waterfall with Zander next to her. "This is exhilarating. "How do I head east?"

"Lean slightly left."

"Got it." It reminded her of snowboarding and how she used the inside of her foot to change directions. Enjoying the view, she straightened her position and reveled in the fact she actually flew. Unreal. Fantastic. Impossible. But here she was, flapping her wings and acting like a bird.

They entered the gnarled grove. The palm leaves twisted and turned, reminding her of green snakes dancing. "These trees are strange."

"This shows you the vortex's power." His voice came out like a soft echo in the wind.

She glanced over at Zander. His blue wings stretched out

as he glided on the air stream. His blond hair slicked back. His smiled wide and practically irresistible.

Should she forgive him?

Had she misconstrued his intention when he asked her to be his mistress?

After learning about his Cupid life, it made sense that he needed to keep his job in the heavenly realm. However, she wasn't sure if she could accept a life with him where she'd only see him in-between assignments.

A tailwind hit her wings. She wobbled and found herself tumbling.

Plummeting, she couldn't think. *I have to do something. Anything. I need to take back my control. If I keep up this speed, I could die. I don't want to die.*

And then Zander swooped her up in his arms. "I've got you."

"You saved me." That had been a close call. What if she had been alone in the enchanted rainforest? Maybe flying had not been such a great idea.

"It's okay, Ivy." His voice crooned. "I'm gonna set you down in one of the trees."

She nodded. Her heart thumped hard and fast in her chest as she held her arms tightly around his neck.

He slowed his speed, floated above the last tree on the left, and drifted down into the top while scattering a cluster of coconuts to the ground.

"I've never been so scared." She bent her knees and carefully sat in a flat spot. Her body trembled. "If you hadn't been there—"

"But I was, and you're safe." He eased in next to her and wrapped his arms around her. "Believe me, hotshot. You'll have this down by the end of the day."

"I don't know."

"You will. You excel at everything you do." He pulled her closer.

"Not everything." Including flying and relationships.

"You're tense." He massaged her shoulders. "Relax, please."

"My world's turned topsy-turvy and inside out. It's rather daunting." The enormity of her morning hit her. "I haven't had time to absorb my magical abilities, and I'm heading back to Moosehead the day after tomorrow."

"I have two more days until my next assignment, and I hope to spend them with you."

"I'm not ready to make any promises. Let's just concentrate on right now." Could she trust her heart if she spent more time with him? Even now, she struggled with the idea of relying on him to help her understand her newfound powers. But he had saved her. That should count for something. She moved out of his arms and plucked a coconut from a bunch.

"I'll take whatever time you'll give me."

"You'll leave me again—just like others have." She had let her guard down with Zander after knowing better.

"I had to go home. I honestly believed that if I went back

to my job, I would forget you. I would move on. You've heard of the old cliché *absence makes the heart grow fonder.* In my case, absence made me woefully unhappy." He placed his hand across his chest. "I acted like an ass, but I'm here now, pouring out my heart for a glimmer of hope."

"You belong with a Cupid woman."

"I belong with you. Last night, as I sat on the surfer's beach listening to the waves roll in and out, the only thing that mattered was you."

She wanted to believe his words. She wanted things to work out. She wanted to be able to love him without waiting for the worst-case scenario. "What happens when your family learns that you are dating me? From what you told me of your life, you had an elitist upbringing. You're expected to find another Cupid with pedigree."

"Relationships with fae are not forbidden."

"Except I am half mortal." She tried to scoot away. He took her hand in his. The simple gesture touched her.

"Cupids believe love is meant to last forever. They believe in soulmates," his voice lowered.

"Don't even go there." The conversation had become far too serious. Her mind couldn't handle relationship talk right now. She could barely handle the fact that she sat on the top of a coconut tree with wings behind her. Handling the idea that she had inherited fae powers seemed surreal. "Let's head back."

"If that's what you'd like." He flashed her a smile. One that didn't reach his eyes.

A part of her longed to forgive and forget.

"You up to flying by yourself?"

"I should be able to manage." She paused. What if she floundered? Free-falling without a parachute had been terrifying. "You will be next to me, right?"

"Of course."

She stood, unfurled her wings to be straight out beside her, and fluttered away. Once soaring again, she let out a long, relieved breath. She could fly confidently with Zander by her side.

CHAPTER 39

Ivy had no idea how long she had been sitting in the wicker chair on Grammy's veranda. At some point, Taffy had jumped onto her lap although she couldn't remember when. Stroking the cat's fur did little to soothe the emotional havoc afflicting her mind. She had magical powers, reminding her of a superhero character in a movie. She could shape-shift into a smaller being.

"Are you all right, dear?" Grammy asked as she took the chair next to her.

"Not really. I just soared above the enchanted forest like a red-tailed hawk. Me, Ivy Venturi." It still seemed farfetched.

"How wonderful." Grammy's eyes twinkled. "I can imagine you're confused."

"More than confused. I usually have everything planned out in sequential order. I know how to get from point A to point B, but right now I don't know what to do. Should I go back to my well-ordered life, or should I embrace my newfound abilities?"

"I can't answer what's best for you. Only you can decide." Grammy's eyes softened. "What's it like to fly?"

"Exhilarating and kind of crazy. I had wings. Pink sparkly wings that flutter and allow me to float upward." She pressed her hand between her shoulder blades together. "They were attached to my shoulders right here."

"How does your magic work?"

"I guess it's stored inside my rose birthmark." Ivy checked her ankle. "It's still hot pink. When I flicked my fingertips dust swirled around me."

"See if it works now?"

Ivy flicked her fingers, and glittery pink dust swirled around her body. In seconds, she shrunk to be the size of a ruler.

"Oh, my." Grammy stared at her. "You are rather small and quite adorable."

"Thanks, I think." Ivy fluttered her wings and floated a few feet about Grammy. "I can fly. I can freaking fly." Earlier today, it seemed like an accident or maybe a dream. Now, she took in the setting. The house appeared huge; the thatched roof gigantic. She slowed her wings, dropped down in her chair, and flicked more dust to change into her human form. Human form?

"I assume you like flying."

"I love it." She thought of how helpful Zander had been

when she first transformed. He had remained by her side, acting as her safety net. She could fly–and so could Zander.

What did she want with him?

"What's wrong?"

There lies the million-dollar question. "There's too much to process." Too much for her brain to decipher.

"I'm assuming that includes your young man?" Grammy raised a brow.

"Yes." Ivy needed to sort things out with him.

"I wish I could help you. I know whenever your grandfather had lots to ponder, he'd go surfing. The ocean seems to have its own power, a power to aid in inner reflection."

Riding a wave. Becoming one with the ocean might bring her answers. "You're brilliant."

"No, dear, I just have years of experience to call upon."

Ivy got up and hugged Grammy. "I love you."

"As I you." Grammy hugged her back.

Tears misted Ivy's eyes. Grammy had always been her rock.

ZANDER CARRIED his rental surfboard into the water. A cluster of surfers positioned themselves about a mile to the south as he entered the water and made his way out. Waves rolled by.

His mind drifted to his conversation with Ivy as he sat on the board with his feet in the water. She still didn't trust him, might never ever fully trust him. At least she had allowed him to escort her to the enchanted rainforest. And learning she was fae meant their relationship might have a better chance of working.

He watched a surfer paddle into a wave, move into a standing position, and take a ride. He'd never surfed before, but it didn't look much different than riding a skateboard. He had this.

The next wave came, and he paddled into the set. His hands grasped the board's sides. He pushed up. His left foot near the tail. His right on the board's center. Like a slap in the face, he tumbled into the cool water. He treaded upward from the pull of the board on his leashed ankle.

Climbing back on, his pulse thudded. No way would a stinking curl of water get the better of him. He waited for two more sets of waves and took the third. Rising, he attempted to get balanced and once again fell into the water.

Holy Hades! Surfing was not as easy as it looked.

Taking the next wave, he carefully rose to a standing position. The curl grabbed him like watery fingers pushing him forward, making him weightless, as if gliding on top of the water and riding inside a liquid tunnel. Spray cooled his whole body. His heart sped. Adrenaline pumped through his veins.

He glanced toward the shore, wobbled, and found himself falling. The tip of the board hit his forehead as he tumbled into the water. Surrounded by coolness, his head throbbed. He couldn't tell which way was up, and then only blackness.

"You okay, mate," a man's voice said as his hand grasped Zander's and moved him towards his board.

"I am now." Zander eased onto his belly and pushed up to be sitting.

"That's a nasty gash on your forehead."

Zander's hand touched something sticky.

Holy Zeus.

Skateboarding might get him bumps and bruises. Nothing like this.

"Let's get you to shore."

"I can make it on my own." Zander's head might be bleeding, but he refused help. He paddled into the next wave on his knees as a wave of dizziness hit. So much for surfing being as easy as a slice of lemon meringue pie. Somehow, he managed to make it to the shore.

And then he spotted Ivy on the beach, running in the sand to his side. "What happened?" She kneeled next to him.

"The board decided to greet my head." He put his board down and sat on it. A group of people had circled around him.

"Looks like the board won." She laughed, shaking her head.

"I suppose. A kiss might make things better." A sympathy kiss seemed pretty pathetic, but he'd take whatever she offered.

She kissed his cheek, and he breathed in her sweet floral scent. His heart beat faster and faster.

"Stand back, everyone." The man pointed to a teenage

girl. "Grab my first aid kit and a couple of water bottles out of my station."

That's when Zander realized the guy in red trunks must be a lifeguard.

The man cleared the crowd, except for Ivy, who stayed by him on the right. "How are you, sir?" His dark eyes focused on Zander.

"I'm all right." Besides being humiliated. After all, Zander should have had this surfing thing down after a couple of tries.

"Are you dizzy?'

A little, not that he'd admit that out loud. He shook his head.

"How many fingers am I holding up?"

That question was utterly ridiculous. "Three."

"Good."

A teenage girl handed the lifeguard his kit and Zander a bottle of water.

"Thanks." He unscrewed the cap and downed the drink. Who knew surfing could make him this thirsty?

"I'm gonna clean your wound." He unwrapped a cloth. "This might sting." The lifeguard wiped something across his forehead.

It burned like Hades. Even though he winced, no way would he make a noise.

Ivy still kneeled next to him with a stone-serious pressed-together mouth and worry in her eyes. She did care.

"It's not as bad as I thought." He rubbed an ointment on

his cut and covered it. "A few butterfly bandages should do the trick. Too bad I don't have any."

"My grandmother should have some back at her place, or she'll do stitches if necessary."

No thank you to getting sewn up. It sounded painful.

"If you're not up to climbing those steps, I can radio for a jeep," the lifeguard said.

"I can make it," he heard himself snarl. A little scratch on his head wouldn't stop him.

"I'll be in my stand if you need anything." The lifeguard held out his hand and shook Zander's.

"I appreciate your help. Thanks."

"You owe, Kahuna, the thanks. He's the one that fished you out of the water." The lifeguard waved over a tanned dark-haired man standing a few feet away.

The words hit Zander. Fished him out of the water. He could have died out there.

Ivy had her arm around Zander's waist. "Can't you use magic to heal yourself?"

"Nope. I didn't inherit restorative powers."

"That's too bad." She brought him up the front porch steps. "Grammy," she called into the house. "Do you have any butterfly bandages? Zander could use a couple on his head."

"Sit down. Be right there."

Ivy chose the chair next to the couch. When she saw

Zander on the beach with blood covering his forehead, her stomach clenched. She might be confused about her feelings for him but never wished for him to be injured.

Grammy came in with a box of supplies. "What happened?"

"My attempt to surf didn't go so well." It bugged him that he got hurt.

"The board got you?" Grammy pulled off the bandage. "Got quite a cut on your forehead."

"I'm fine." Typical male. He was determined to act macho.

Grammy cleansed his laceration, added ointment, and pressed four butterfly bandages to push the wound together. "Leave the bandages on for the next day. I'll give you a jar of my special healing salve. Starting the day after tomorrow, dab some on twice a day for the next week. You'll be good as new as long as you stay out of the water."

"And I was hoping Ivy would give me a surfing lesson before I left."

"Not this time. Next time … if she invites you back." Grammy winked. The tease. She knew full well that the likelihood of Ivy and Zander becoming a couple was precarious. "Oh my. It's already four. I've got to deliver fresh pineapple to my friend. Left some in the fridge. Help yourself. Pineapple is known to aid in healing." Grammy picked up a covered bowl from the counter. "Probably won't be back for an hour or two."

Zander chuckled. "I think she wants to give us privacy—not that I'm complaining."

"I'm sorry you were injured. Just don't read more into it." Processing the fact that she could fly had been enough to contemplate

"Okay. How do you feel about your magical abilities?"

"Flying is awesome, but I would have to stay here to keep on doing that. And I need to get back to work the day after tomorrow."

"Couldn't you delay your trip?"

"I promised my boss I'd be back. I allowed myself a day after I get back because jet lag takes a toll on my concentration." She needed some normalcy to manage her oh-so-chaotic-turn-of-affairs.

"What if I told you I have a way for you to avoid jet lag.

"If it involves magic, no thank you."

"I'll honor your wishes." He got up from the couch and kneeled in front of her chair and reached for her hand. "Would you be okay if I visited you in Moosehead?"

"Maybe?" She should have said no. With her muddled mind, the last thing she needed was to add him into the mix.

"Great." Giving her a lopsided grin, he was far too sexy.

Boy, was she in trouble!

CHAPTER 40

Friday, September 11th

ZANDER ENTERED the café and searched for Ivy. After leaving her on the island, it had taken him two weeks to get her to agree to meet. He spotted her near the back corner of the room and waved. Walking toward her, she sipped a glass of red wine.

His hands shook as he gave a bouquet of hibiscus to her and sat in the opposite booth. "Hey."

"Hi."

"You look gorgeous." He longed to pull her black hair out of the severe bun and run his fingers through the silky tresses.

"Thanks."

"How are you?" He had talked to her on the phone a total of three times, and those calls had been stiff.

"Well, and you?" She flashed a smile that didn't reach her eyes and picked up a carafe of wine. "Would you like some?"

"Please."

She poured liquid in his glass and sat ramrod straight in her chair.

If only he could get back what they once had. "I've missed you."

She shrugged. The waitress came up, and they ordered.

"I still can't believe I can fly," she said in a soft voice.

"I'm happy you can. Besides water sports and skateboarding, it gives us one more thing in common." He grabbed the basket of bread, took out a slice and buttered it. "We're good together."

"What do you really want?"

"I want you to forgive me. I want us to be a couple again. I want to be with you." He needed her love. "How about you?"

"I don't know. I like it here, but a part of me would like to be that little fae flittering in the enchanted forest." She held his gaze. "What should I do?"

"Only you can answer that question. I'm hoping I can be a part of your life." He sipped his wine. "I told my parents about you." He had approached his mom first, unsure what she would say when he explained that Ivy was a fae. Instead, his mom had hugged him, saying she wanted him to be happy.

"You're breaking it off for good. You could've just texted me." Her tone came out choppy.

"They'd like to meet you." His mom's insistence had been a shock.

"Even though I'm a hybrid."

"They'd like to meet the woman who has captured my heart." He may be taking things a bit fast, but he didn't wish to hold any information from her.

"I'm not ready to make their acquaintance."

"I get it, but I just had to tell you. I'm committed to make our crazy life work somehow." He reached for her hand. "If you ever forgive me."

"I have."

Joy surged through his heart.

Once they finished dinner, they strolled along the street. The summer crowds were gone. Only a scattering of people were out. The weather had gotten chillier, and the wind kicked up slightly. Ivy shivered.

He took off his jacket and put it around her shoulders. "Mind if we sit here a minute." He pointed to a nearby bench.

"Not at all." She eased into the bench.

He sat next to her. "I love you, Ivy."

Her eyes widened with surprise.

He leaned over and brushed his lips against hers. "I fell in love with you the moment you picked out those Etnie tennis shoes." He kissed her, slow and gentle.

"You're such a romantic."

"And you love every minute." He kissed her again. "One of these days, you're going to admit you love me, too."

"One of these days, I just might do that." She initiated the kiss.

Ivy had forgiven him. She might not totally trust him, but eventually, he'd win her confidence.

CHAPTER 41

Saturday, November 12th

IVY PACED BACK and forth in her condo. For the past two months, Zander spent almost every weekend with her. He wore down her resistance with flowers, a diamond bracelet. And last weekend, she finally admitted she loved him.

Big mistake!

He talked her into meeting his parents. She would be visiting his parent's estate. Their estate in Cupid's Corner.

She texted: *I can't go.*

You'll be fine. I promise.

I'm ill. Sick to my stomach. This was true. Her stomach churned.

The doorbell rang. "Open up, Ivy. It's just nerves."

She turned the doorknob.

He entered and pulled her into his arms. “Relax. I love you, and so will my parents.”

“And if they don’t?” She just knew something would go wrong.

“Quit fretting. You ready to change into an adorable fairy?”

“Just go on without me.” It wasn’t like Ivy to be this nervous. Usually, she took things head-on or more like by the horns. But the idea of traveling to another realm to meet Zander’s parents terrified her.

“Not on your life.” He led her outside to his red beamer, opened the door, and leaned down to give her a heated kiss. “Just remember, I love you.”

“Where are we going?” She had to know.

“A sunbeam not far from the airport.” He got in and revved the engine.

They arrived at a secluded spot. She swirled her magical dust, shrunk to be a foot tall with wings on her back and wearing a sparkly pink dress and satin slippers.

A second later, his dust swirled again, and he shrunk to be an inch or two taller than her. “Now for our ride.” First, a chariot appeared, then a winged Pegasus.

“This is incredible.” She petted the animal’s nose.

“Only the best for you.” He assisted her into the chariot. “Unfurl your wings so they don’t get in the way. Make sure to hold onto the railing when we take off. This Pegasus moves fast.”

"Is it too late to change my mind?" As much as she wished to experience the ride, the idea of meeting his parents made her tremble.

"Yes." He kissed her cheek. "Hold on tight. Pegasus, take off." He flicked the reins, and the horse ascended upward. The airport became a tiny dot and disappeared.

Her hands kept a death grip on the bar as she zoomed upward into the clouds at what might be the speed of light. The animal neighed and flew through thick, cumulus clouds. The white fog made it hard to see her own hands. Then the clouds grew thin as they soared above snowcapped mountains.

"Descend," he called. The horse slowed its speed, and she could see a lake surrounded by grassy meadows and colorful flowers.

"What's the lake called?"

"Aphrodite," he said. "Her castle is to the East."

According to Greek mythology, Aphrodite was the goddess of love. It figured a Cupid community would name a lake after her, but a castle seemed surreal. The frosted heart-shaped windows glistened. She counted ten pink spires on top.

"Next time we visit, we'll go to the lake, or we could go rafting on the Fates River."

If there was a next time. Right now, she had to get through meeting the family. Her stomach did a loop de loop.

"Cupid's Corner is to the south. My apartment is the last one to the west."

"Can we just go there and skip your family?" she gasped. Jitters filled her soul. What had she been thinking? No way could she make it through today.

"Quit stressing. Everyone will love you." He placed his hand above hers. "I love you." He jiggled the reins and circled a large estate, a mansion really with what looked like a stable behind the big house. Grass and flowers made the scene picturesque. Shrubs separated the mansion from the neighboring homes. The animal landed in the clearing in front of the main building.

"Welcome to my family's estate." He got out and reached for her hand.

"Wow." She remained paralyzed, gripping the railing like it were her lifesaver. Ridiculous.

Well, Ivy had dealt with demanding clients before. She squared her shoulders, took Zander's arm, and headed between the massive columns which adorned the front veranda. He parted the cloud-covered doorway.

The idea that a cloud could be used for a door made her laugh. Magic in this realm was certainly unique.

Ushered inside the foyer, she checked out the quartzite flooring and was pretty sure it was embedded with bits of sapphires. Showy.

The living room happened to be about four times as large as hers. Queen Anne style chairs covered with pink and red floral designs were placed near a marble fireplace and next to a tufted red velvet chair. Voices drifted from another room.

"Hey, Mom," Zander said to a petite blonde woman who seemed to just appear from the other room. "This is my girlfriend, Ivy."

"It's nice to meet you." His mother smiled. "Everyone's in the dining room. We're just about to eat."

Knowing Zander was a vegetarian, she hoped his family followed suit because she could handle eating vegetables but not something weird like turtle soup or frog's legs. Gagging in front of Zander's family would be embarrassing.

Her feet walked like bricks as he led her into the dining room.

She closed her eyes for a second to compose her silly angst. She could do this.

Her mouth dropped as she entered the dining room. The room looked twice, no, three times as big as her living room and kitchen combined. China and diamond-plated silverware adorned the table. At least a dozen people sat at an oval table made of redwood. As Zander pulled out a chair close to the end and sat next to her, all eyes were on her.

"Everyone, this is Ivy."

She gave a nervous wave and picked up her red napkin embroidered with a white cherub archer.

"Welcome." A man with laugh lines and Zander's blue eyes said from the end of the table. "In case you're wondering, I'm his dad."

"Nice to meet you." Ivy could swear her voice came out raspy. And that was just the start. She met Zander's brothers, his sister-in-laws, three nephews, one niece, four of his cousins, and his aunt and uncle. Overwhelmed would be considered an understatement. She pasted on a smile and pretended like meeting a group of Cupids was a normal task.

His father waved his hand, and glasses of ambrosia floated down to the table. He toasted, "To friends and family."

She sipped the sweet drink and glanced over at Zander.

He winked.

Okay, this dinner wasn't that bad.

"Let's eat," one of the brothers said.

His father flicked his fingertips and created some sort of tossed salad and floated the bowl around to everyone. She took a small portion, not sure how her stomach might digest food in this realm.

"How'd you two meet?" a blonde girl who might be his cousin asked.

"I was on assignment in her town and just had to ask her out," Zander said and put his hand on her leg.

Instead of being comforted, she wished she could crawl under the table. Better yet, she wished she could disappear.

"What town?" his brother asked.

"Does it matter?" Zander's voice had a snap to it.

"No." The same brother stared at her. "Are you considering moving to Cupid's Corner, Ivy?"

"Not at the moment." *Most likely never,* she would've said but figured she'd keep her discussion curt.

"Has Zander shown you his blueprints for the house on this estate?" his mother said softly.

Talk about a blatant hint. "I can't say he has."

"You should show it to her. It's quite a home." His father sat taller like he was proud of his son.

"He planned to have it built for his ex, Cami," his brother added. "But they broke up."

His mother glared at the brother. "Hope you all like my mushroom stroganoff. It's a new recipe made with bow-tie pasta." His mother flicked her fingertips, and pink dust swirled to create a large dish of food which was passed around the table.

Ivy added a small portion and took a bite. "This is delicious."

"Thank you." His mother blustered at the compliment.

"It's terrific, Mom," Zander said, and others nodded in agreement.

"Uncle Andre, how was your trip to Africa?" someone asked.

"Delightful. I knew elephants were huge but seeing one in person is rather amazing. So were the hippos. We took a boat excursion, in human form of course, and I got to see how they wiggle their ears in the water while swimming." He took his wife's hand. "It turned out to be a wonderful second honeymoon."

The wife blushed. "You should go if you ever get a chance."

"I'd rather see Scotland. I've heard the fae population is quite friendly. Plus, the countryside is spectacular, or so it seems on Outlander," one of the sister-in-laws said.

Obviously, the Cupid had watched the series.

When everyone was done eating, the dishes were floated into what Ivy assumed was the kitchen. The magic was far too surreal.

"Any takers for strawberry mousse?" his uncle asked.

"You have to try it, Ivy.," Zander said.

Two hours later, Zander brought Ivy into his apartment.

"That was intense." She plopped on the couch.

"You passed with flying colors." He moved in next to her, placed his arm around her shoulders, and pulled her close.

"Do you really have a blueprint for a house on your parent's property?" She crossed her legs, her eyes guarded.

"It's on the counter. Do you want to see it?"

"Don't think I'd ever consider living here, but I'd like to see what details you'd pick for your place."

Knowing Ivy, he doubted she could be happy in this realm, and he couldn't give up being an archer. There had to be a middle ground where they could meet. He got up and handed her the plans.

"Four bedrooms. Three baths. Interesting. I like the open living room, but do you need such a huge formal dining room?"

"If I lived here, yes. You've only met part of my family. Sometimes more of my aunts, uncles, and cousins come to town." He leaned over and kissed her tenderly. "I've got a crazy idea."

She caught his eyes and held them.

"At first light, we leave Cupid's Corner and spend the rest of the weekend in Rhapsody?" That way, he could enjoy her in her fae form but leave this realm that made her less than comfortable.

"Yes, please." She sighed, her gorgeous eyes sparkling.

He pulled her into his arms and carried her into his bed. "But for the rest of tonight, let's enjoy being alone at my place."

CHAPTER 42

Ivy couldn't help smiling as she knocked on Grammy's door with Zander at her side.

"Come in," Grammy called.

She and Zander stepped inside. Grammy's expression was priceless. Her mouth dropped, and her eyes widened. "Ivy? What are you doing here? You're supposed to be in Cupid's Corner." She wiped her hands on her apron and embraced her in a hug.

"Already did that. We decided to make an impromptu trip." Ivy laughed. "It seems Zander's Cupid powers have some advantages. It took us minutes to ride a sunbeam here from his realm."

"How wonderful." Grammy's eyes crinkled. "Aloha, Zander. Come on over and give me a hug."

With Grammy being only five feet, if that, Zander seemed to tower over her.

"Let's sit outside." Grammy took her usual chair.

She and Zander chose the porch swing with his arm over the back. It amazed her how natural it felt to have him next to her.

"How'd it go with Zander's parents?" Grammy asked, cutting to the chase.

"Well," Zander said.

"Not bad. They asked if I'd be moving to Cupid's Corner." Ivy had managed to keep her calm while she wanted to say, *"Hell, no!"*

"Are you?" Grammy raised a brow.

"As if." Glancing over at Zander, she noticed his eye tick. Did he hope to talk her into living in a world where she would never truly fit?

"You seem to be making it work in Moosehead."

"We are." Zander pulled her closer. "I'm one lucky guy."

"And don't you forget it." Ivy joked while deep inside, she wondered how they could continue with their relationship. Their worlds were far too different.

"Have you two eaten? I can whip up some eggs and fruits," Grammy said.

"No need. We had breakfast before we left." Zander smiled at Ivy.

Her heart went pitter-patter every time she saw his handsome face.

"If you two are planning to go surfing, I'll keep my first aid kit handy," Grammy chuckled.

"Maybe later. I'm hoping to take Ivy back to the enchanted rainforest." He turned to face her. "If that's okay?"

The fact that he asked meant a great deal to her. She'd learned to trust him, which still scared her, but she had to let him in and push past her deep-seated insecurities. "I'd like that."

"Will you be back in time for dinner?"

"We should be," Zander said.

"Have fun." Grammy got up and walked them to the door.

They strolled hand in hand along the path. "I like this island."

"So do I." Although she hadn't spent much time here over the last few years, still the island made her happy.

"Have you ever considered living here full time?" Zander asked as they reached the cavern entrance to the enchanted rainforest.

"My job is in Moosehead along with my friends." She would have her law degree soon, and her boss promised her a partnership in the firm. She couldn't walk away from that.

"I get it." He said with a soft tone. "Ready to get your wings."

"Absolutely." She flicked her fingertips, hot pink dust surrounded her body, and she shrank into her fae size. Since she adored flying, living here would allow her to practice her magic, but how could she tie living here with her work?

"I thought we'd go for a swim underneath the waterfall." Zander had transformed into his Cupid shape.

Funny, she'd gotten used to him with blue wings and couldn't decide if she liked him better in human form or as a Cupid. Like—she was hopelessly in love with Zander Eros. Even crazier—she'd just visited his Cupid parents and survived.

They flew up through the top of the cavern holding hands.

"Have I told you how much I like flying with you?" Zander asked.

"No, you haven't." She hadn't yet flown without him, but someday she would need to go on her own. Glancing down, she spotted the waterfall and then the grassy meadow where they would land. Only birds and dragonflies seemed to be here, and she attributed their isolation due to being early in the morning. She let go of his hand, slowed her wings, and floated down next to Zander.

He turned to face her, pulled her in his arms, and kissed her with such sweetness. "I love you, Ivy."

She pushed him away. "I'm going swimming." She flicked her fingertips. Her magical dust swirled around her body and replaced her short dress with a pink polka dot bikini.

Zander whistled. He had changed into red swim trunks. She'd seen his chest bare countless times, but that didn't stop her from gasping in pleasure at his toned abs and muscular chest. Her boyfriend had a spectacular body.

She ran into the water until it reached her chest.

He came up behind and wrapped his arms around her waist. "This is nice." His warm breath tickled her neck. His simple touch made her core heat up.

"It is," she sighed and leaned back into him. The frothy cascade of water roared from several yards away, causing ripples in the pool. A rainbow shimmered where the falls met the water. Paradise aptly describes the place.

"You up to swimming behind the falls? It looks like there's a secluded spot there."

Ivy nodded. Zander's sense of adventure matched her own.

They took off. The cool water surrounded her body as she moved her arms and legs. They reached the falls and swam underneath and back a bit further to a ledge. She pulled herself up.

Zander sat beside her. His wet hair slick against his scalp. "I wouldn't mind making this my home base."

"You'd live behind a waterfall?"

"No, silly. I'd have a house built on Rhapsody Island," he took her hand.

"That does sound lovely."

"It would be if I got to share it with you," his tone came out low and dreamy.

Was he serious? Her mind whirled with the possibilities. Could she give up her life in Moosehead to be with him here? "Your home is in Cupid's Corner."

"Not anymore. I know this is crazy. We've only been

together about five months, but I can't see myself with anyone else. I'm serious about you, Ivy. You're my soulmate."

She held her breath for a beat as he gazed at her. Then his mouth brushed against hers. His lips were warm and welcoming. Her arms roped around his neck. She loved kissing him.

"What if we lived here and in Moosehead? With my help, you can take sunbeams back and forth between both places." He nuzzled her neck.

"I mean, I could do most of my work on the internet." What he suggested almost seemed doable. Maybe. "But how will I explain this to my friends?"

"We'll figure it out. I bet Granny has some good ideas?"

"Probably." She still couldn't see it.

"As long as we're together, we can work out anything." He massaged her shoulders, and she relaxed into him. "We can spend time here, and you can teach me to surf. Eventually, you'll teach our cherubs."

Whoa! Her heart skittered. "Did you just say cherubs?"

"Ivy, I want kids with you. A boy and girl when the time comes."

The need to flee hit her. Get away and keep on running. He must've sensed this because he held her waist.

"Don't leave me, Ivy. I get you're scared. I'm a little freaked out by the intensity of our relationship, but it's real. You know it's real." He cleared his throat. "Every day I'm with you, I find myself loving you even more."

She could relate. The more time she spent with him, the more she loved him.

"Marry me." He reached his swim trunks pocket and produced a small red box.

She froze, unable to say a word. For most of her life, she'd watched her mother struggle after her marriages collapsed. But this was Zander.

She stared at a heart-shaped ring with pink opals outlined with red rubies. The ring had been created with her in mind. He really did love her.

"I didn't mean to shock you. I know this is fast. You don't have to give me an answer right now. Take all the time you need. Just promise me you'll consider my proposal." His tone came out squeaky as he slipped the box into his pocket.

All her life, she had been afraid to trust, but Zander just poured out his heart. They had a lot of obstacles to settle, but she wanted them to work. Tears filled her eyes.

"I love you." She kissed his cheek.

"Thank the gods, you still do." He leaned down, his tongue teased the corner of her mouth, and he deepened the kiss and caused the most delightful tingle on her lips.

"Would you mind if we headed back to Grammy's?" She needed some clarity.

"No."

They flew back without talking. The marriage idea had thrown her for a loop, and she figured that her non-answer weighed on him.

CHAPTER 43

Zander plunked down against a coconut tree on the beach. He'd blown it with Ivy. He couldn't lose her because he'd been impatient.

"Hey, Zander." Veronica kneeled next to him. "What has dragged you down?" In human form, she didn't look quite as delicate; however, she still had those dark, inquisitive eyes.

"You don't want to know." He'd rather just sit here alone and contemplate his next steps.

"Try me." She sat next to him. "I'm a good listener and a pretty good problem solver. I'm guessing it has to do with your girlfriend. Did she break up with you?"

"Not exactly." He wished she'd quit pushing.

"What exactly happened?" She folded her arms around her knees.

Should he tell her? Well, he did need a sounding board

and didn't know anyone else on this island besides Ivy and Grammy. "Things were going great. I even took Ivy to meet my parents."

"That's a pretty big step. How'd she manage?"

Zander laughed. "She got pretty stressed before we arrived at the house, but once she went inside, she did just fine." He'd been proud of how she won over the family.

"Then what's the issue?"

"I asked her to marry me." Deep down, it bugged him that Ivy hadn't said yes.

"And she turned you down. No wonder you're sad." Veronica patted his arm. "I'm sorry."

"She didn't say no."

"What did she say?" She raised a brow.

"I love you." Ivy loved him. That should count for something.

"Give her time. She's a woman, and your proposal surprised her." Veronica stood and put her hands on her hips. "How long have you been dating?'

"Close to five months."

"You're a fast rascal. An alpha man who knows what he wants and goes after it. You got any brothers." She winked.

"Two older ones. Married." To traditional Cupid wives. Zander had wanted that, but after meeting Ivy, he preferred somebody less conventional.

Veronica checked her watch. "Gotta run. Good luck with your girlfriend."

Zander let out a long breath.

"YOU'RE BACK ALREADY." Grammy looked over the top of her book while seated in her chair on the porch.

"Yes." Ivy took the wicker chair next to her.

"Where's Zander?"

Ivy shrugged. She had no idea where he went.

"I know that look. What's wrong?"

Grammy would get it out of her eventually, so she might as well give in. "Zander asked me to marry him."

"I'm not surprised. The boy's crazy about you."

"We'll never survive."

"Do you love him?" Grammy gave her a wistful look.

"Yes." She loved Zander. Her heart was all in, but her mind reminded her this relationship had been a foolish notion.

"The way you look at him tells me your love is meant to last. I believe the real issue is that he's a Cupid." Grammy and her uncanny intuition.

"I can't live in his realm."

"Did he ask you to put your life behind and move up there?"

"No. But his parents did. Plus, he showed me a blueprint for a house he had planned to build on their estate." A blueprint he had designed for him and his ex-fiancé. Not that Ivy would mention the ex to her grandmother.

"Zander's a big boy. He can make up his own mind. What did the two of you talk about before he proposed?" Grammy wore a sweet smile. A smile that said she had a reason for the question.

"He would consider making Rhapsody his home base. He also suggested living both here and in Moosehead." Actually, the suggestion had been rather appealing. "Then he talked about having cherubs."

"You'll make a great mother." She put her hand over Ivy's.

"Grammy." Ivy wasn't having children.

"Just because you had a rough time growing up doesn't mean your children would. Isn't It time you had this discussion with your mother? Tell her about your powers. Make her talk about your father."

"Doesn't she already suspect I have powers?"

"Probably. But leaving, she had hoped the magic would never develop. She did this because she wanted you to have a normal life. In her own way, she was trying to protect you."

Ivy couldn't help rolling her eyes. "I know. I'm going to call her right now."

"Good for you, dear. I'll let you get to your call." Grammy picked up her book while eyeing Ivy over the top.

Ivy walked inside. Showtime!

ZANDER ARRIVED at five o'clock wearing Bermuda shorts and a light blue Hawaiian shirt that matched his eyes. "Is dinner still on?" he asked while pushing back his shoulders, ready for a challenge. The challenge being her.

"Not for another hour."

He gave her another lei, and she put it around her neck.

"You look beautiful. Wanna take a walk." He offered his hand, and she allowed him to help her up. "I missed you this afternoon."

She expected him to kiss her cheek, but he kept a distance between them. "I talked to my mom today."

"About me?"

"Not right away. First, we spoke about her love for my father. She wasn't surprised I inherited his fae powers."

He shortened his strides and inched a bit closer to her.

"She told me if she had to do things over, she would have married my father again. She said when you find true love, hold onto it because your likelihood of ever finding that kind of love is slim." Ivy took a breath. Her mother also said Ivy had done a great job helping raise her siblings. "What she said hit a cord. If you still wish to marry me, my answer is yes."

"Hold that thought." He got down on one knee and pulled the red box out of his backpack. "Ivelisse Venturi, we will make a great team. I don't care if we choose to live on Rhapsody or Moosehead or Timbuktu for that matter, as long as we're together. Will you marry me?"

"I will." As unbelievable as it seemed, she would be getting hitched.

Zander stood and pulled her into his arms and swung her around. "Soon, you will be Mrs. Ivelisse Eros."

"Venturi-Eros." She wasn't about to give up her heritage but didn't mind adding his sir name.

"Whatever makes you happy." He kissed her senseless,

"I'm thinking of a June wedding." She smirked.

He counted the months on his fingers. "Seven months is a long time, but I can wait. Our first date was on June 13th." He pulled up the calendar. "June 14th is a Saturday."

"Or we could elope. Your family will expect the wedding to be in Cupid's Corner." Her pulse sped, and she pulled out of his arms. "This wedding isn't such a great idea."

"You already said yes. You can't back down now." He secured his arm around her shoulder. "I love you. You love me. What about marrying right here on the beach?"

"Are you sure the decision won't cause a rift with your parents?" He and his family were close.

"We've got until June to ease them into the idea. Plus, I know you'll want Grammy there along with your family and friends."

"They're humans. Won't that be awkward?" She seriously doubted their marriage would be acceptable.

"Leave it up to me to smooth out the details with my mom. Once she's onboard, everything else will be smooth flying."

"Don't you mean sailing?"

He shrugged. "Are we settled?"

"We are."

He plucked a magenta-colored orchid from a nearby plant, placed the flower behind her ear, and trailed his thumb under her chin. "I can't believe you're my fiancé." He pulled her into his arms and kissed her for the longest time. She felt charged. Energized. Content. "Let's go tell Grammy the good news."

They walked arm in arm back to the hut with Ivy humming the song "June Bride" from the old movie, *Seven Brides for Seven Brothers.*

EPILOGUE

June 14th, Rhapsody Island

The bedroom got pretty cramped with Ivy's friends and sisters surrounding her in Grammy's bedroom. Her four bridesmaids wore short dresses in hot pink. Her favorite color. Many people had traveled far to be with her on her special day.

In her grandmother's bedroom, Penelope and Sammy worked on her hair. She had opted to let it flow with French braids connecting the back.

"We're finished." Penelope held up a hand mirror and showed her where they had weaved in plumeria throughout the braid.

"I helped with that one." Her three-year-old niece Noni pointed.

"It looks perfect. You ready to be my flower girl?" Ivy

kneeled to be eye level.

"Yes, Auntie Ivy." Noni gave Ivy an innocent smile.

"She's been talking non-stop about her important job." Her sister Goldie said and hugged Ivy. "I'm happy for you."

"Thanks."

"You've found a good guy." Her youngest sister Hannah embraced her.

"I have." Zander had told her enough times they were soulmates that she finally believed the notion.

"It's crowded in here, so I'll get Noni out of your hair." Goldie picked up her daughter. A blonde, just like her sister.

"We'll be waiting for you outside while you dress," Hannah said and walked out behind Goldie.

"Let's get you into this gorgeous gown. I love the shimmering pink overlay." Sammy was adorable with her baby bump. She unzipped the wedding gown, and Ivy stepped into her strapless knee-length dress.

"Hold in while I zip," Penelope said and had the gown adjusted in seconds.

Ivy twirled, allowing the bell-shaped skirt to billow.

"Zander won't be able to take his eyes off you," Sammy gushed. "You look like a princess."

"She sure does." Her mother walked in, dabbing her eyes with a tissue.

"Don't start, mom. I'm not about to smear my makeup." She fought off happy tears. In less than thirty minutes, she would be marrying Zander. It still seemed unbelievable.

"Now for the shoes." Penelope slipped on her one-inch sandal with shimmering pink rhinestones.

Sammy helped with the left. "Only you would go for such bling. By the way, I love the pink polka-dotted fingernails and toenails."

Ivy's face heated. She recalled wearing a pink polka-dot bikini when Zander first proposed.

"You need something borrowed and old." Grammy walked in. "Would you mind wearing the necklace your grandfather gave to me on my wedding night?" She held out a string of pearls.

"I'd love to wear them." Nostalgia hit her as Grammy secured the clasp. These pearls were a part of her family heritage.

"I have something old and borrowed—the pearls. Something new—my dress and shoes. Now I need something blue."

Penelope pulled out a garter with blue lace from her bag and grinned. "I thought you might say that." She placed it just above her knee.

"Your father would have been proud to see this day," her mom sighed.

"I wish I could remember him."

"Whenever you smile, you remind me of him."

Ivy clenched her hands in an effort to ward off any tears. "Is Jed here yet? He's famous for arriving late."

"I'm sitting in the living room," he called. "And I'm never late."

"Never?"

"Let's get the show on the road." Penelope ushered her out the door.

"You look incredible," Ivy said to her brother. His cropped hair matched his black tie and contrasted his white tux.

"So do you, sis." He took both her hands and gazed directly at her. "You sure you want to marry Zander?"

"Absolutely." She loved him more than she ever thought possible.

It took less than five minutes for the group to make their way to the top of the stone steps leading to the beach. Zander's two brothers greeted the party.

"We've got an anxious bridegroom waiting for you." The oldest brother smiled showing dimples just like Zander. He turned to Grammy. "I'm in charge of escorting you to your seat." He held out his arm, and she watched her sweet grandmother walk down the steps.

"Ready, ma'am," the other brother said and held out his arm for her mom.

She could see Zander waiting near his uncle but not very clearly. His uncle had insisted on officiating, and after meeting the Cupid, she considered him to be the right choice. His family had supported her decision to marry on the island.

She had expected his mother to object about having to shift into human form, not sound excited to have the wedding at this exotic location. While she hinted that they should move to Cupid's Corner, she hadn't pushed.

Goldie went down the steps first holding her daughter's hand, followed by Hannah, Penelope, and Sammy.

Then it was her turn. "Ready, sis?" Jed asked.

"I am." She held his arm and started down, glad that she had opted for one-inch sandals and a shorter dress. Chairs were set up in lines of ten on each side of the aisle covered with a white cloth.

One of the locals played the wedding march on a ukulele, and everyone stood and faced her. There must've been a hundred faces staring at her. She gripped her brother's arm.

Then her eyes met Zander's, and she swooned. His grin widened, and love shone in his eyes. She could swear she walked on air the rest of the way, even though she knew that would be impossible on Earth.

Her brother handed her off. "Take good care of her."

"Always," Zander crooned, wearing a sexy grin that made her heart beat faster.

"We are gathered here to join this man and woman together in matrimony," his uncle said and kept talking, but all Ivy noticed was how handsome Zander looked in a white tux and a pink bowtie that matched her gown.

"I do," Zander said and winked at her.

Oh no. She'd better pay attention. "Do you take Zander to be your lawfully wedded husband?"

"I do," her voice squeaked.

And they were exchanging vows and rings in what seemed like a blur.

"You may kiss the bride," his uncle said.

Zander leaned down and seared his lips against hers and kissed her with passion. When he pulled away, he said, "We did it."

"Yes, we did." A year ago, she had been on her first date with Zander. Despite plenty of obstacles, they were now married

"I'd like to introduce Mr. and Mrs. Zander Eros," his uncle said.

"I like the sound of that." He squeezed her hand as they walked down the aisle.

"Venturi-Eros." She countered.

"Life with a firebrand wife will always be interesting." He swooped her up into his arms and kissed her senseless.

The End

Time to Save a Cowboy

If you enjoyed FIREBRAND'S CUPID, you might want to read TIME TO SAVE A COWBOY from my Western Time Travel Series.

The Cowboy Doesn't Deserve to HANG

Captivated by the story of a cowboy hanged as a horse thief in 1890, Mia Kellogg travels back in time with only thirty days to save an innocent man.

Dusty Mann is determined to buy his own ranch.

He doesn't need a modern, straightforward woman to barrel into his life or knock his plans off track.

But Mia steals his heart—and then says she's from the future.

Read an excerpt from TIME TO SAVE A COWBOY

In front of Mia, a gentleman in a dark suit and top hat assisted a lady into her carriage seat. The driver positioned himself to her left and picked up the reins. His horse neighed.

Mia shifted back a few steps, giving the horse plenty of room as she leaned her elbows against a railing behind her. The buggy took off leaving thin ruts in the powdery dirt.

Hot air raced down her neck. Something hit the back of her head, jerking her forward, pushing her, making her stumble into the street. She gained her footing. Spun around. Her arms pinwheeled. "Stop tha—"

Her words clogged her throat, cut off her breath.

A horse, oh no, a horse.

She stared at its large, triangular brown head inches from her face. No, not large. Gigantic. Her heart tripped in her chest; her legs became immovable.

Its nostrils flared, its obsidian-colored eyes widened.

She tried to move, but her limbs became rigid, her feet cemented in place. The horse stomped one hoof against the ground and swished its tail against its flank. A thousand pounds of imposing beast sniffed the air.

She stood frozen, watching its nostrils flair and flatten, flare and flatten. "Get, get back."

The horse's mouth opened, and it bared teeth the size of playing cards.

Move, she told herself. Move, before it stomps on you.

The horse let out a high-pitched snort and threw its head up.

She was gone, racing down the street, sprinting up the hotel's wide wooden staircase, straight through an open door, running fast. Fear propelled her like a slingshot.

She charged inside and plowed into a solid object with an umph.

"Slow down." Large hands steadied her and released its hold. The man stepped away.

At only five-foot-two, she stared straight at his massive shoulders. This guy must spend hours at the gym. Okay, she had to quit gawking at his chest. She gazed up as he took off his worn-leather Stetson.

He gave her a lopsided grin. "Somethin' troubling you?"

"No." Not wanting to seem like an idiot, she stoned her expression, while her knees wobbled.

"You're kinda pale. Best you sit a spell." He placed his hands on her shoulders and guided her to an overstuffed couch near a brick fireplace. Heat sizzled through her gown's fabric, and her insides tingled.

"Excuse me." The cowboy flagged a waitress in a long black dress and white apron. "I'd be obliged if you brought this lady some water." He relaxed in an adjacent armchair and flashed her a brazen smile. "Never had a beautiful gal barrel into me. What's the hurry, miss?"

"Um, you see, this horse, it scared me. The horse, um, was huge, enormous." Sounding stupid, she concentrated on a multicolored glass-blown vase on the side table and rearranged the orange poppies to be in front of the violets and lupines.

"Must've been one of Ben's Belgian draft horses," he said, and she noticed his russet brown hair touched the top of his shirt collar.

The server handed her a glass of water. She took a sip. "It's warm."

"No surprise. This is the desert." The cowboy's drawl didn't seem practiced.

"I'm not as freaked as—" She looked at him, really looked at him, and recognized those wide-set gray eyes from somewhere. "You look familiar."

"I'd remember meeting a pretty gal like you." His smile lit up his handsome face, and her heart fluttered.

She focused on the people at the front desk. A clerk slid a key to a man, and he left with a lady in a long chiffon dress. Most likely people from the train.

A heavy-set woman approached her. "I'm Jenny Hayes. My husband, Bob, and I manage the hotel."

"Mia Kellogg." She held out her hand.

Jenny gave her a sideways glance.

Why wouldn't she shake her hand? Must be a germaphobe.

"Saw Dusty walk you in. Did the heat get to you?"

"Maybe a little. I'm fine now." Mia examined his features. His tan complexion set off his wolf gray eyes. He was a ringer to the cowboy from the picture in the antique shop. "Your name's Dusty?"

He straightened and rewarded her with a mischievous grin. "Yep."

"His given name's Harold Mann, but folks have been calling him Dusty since he was knee high to a grasshopper." Jenny butted in. She must be related to him somehow. "What brings you to our town?"

"A short vacation."

"Well, you certainly chose an ideal time for your stay. Tomorrow's our monthly ball." Jenny's cheeks reddened.

Now Mia was confused. She and Birdie had tickets for the Daggett dance. Maybe she got the name of the town wrong. Still, if her relatives were here, she should have seen them by now. "Could I borrow your phone and call my cousin?" Mia asked, anxious to talk with someone she knew.

"Golly, we don't have a telephone here. Our general store is the only business in town that has one. The shop's closed 'till morning," Jenny said.

Mia's throat got tight. Only one phone in town. This took the turn-of-the-last-century thing a bit far.

"I imagine you're famished, miss. May I find you a table in the dining room?"

"Please." Starved, at least her stomach didn't rumble.

Jenny turned to Dusty. "Will you be joining Miss Kellogg?"

Mia expected him to refuse politely. Not say, "I'd be honored." He stood and offered his arm. His scent of leather and masculinity made her lean closer. Wrong response for a guy she'd just met.

Jenny led the two of them through the spacious ballroom.

Mia's right foot hit a slick, polished spot on the hardwood flooring. "Oh no."

Dusty tightened his grasp on her arm. "Careful, darlin'."

Was her lightheadedness from lack of food or ... was it him? She took small mindful steps to their linen covered table. Mindful of the waxed floor. Mindful of clutching his muscular biceps.

"Here you go." He pulled out her chair. His gray eyes darkened when he looked at her. He appeared well-mannered, but she wondered if his kisses would hold a bad boy edge. She couldn't believe she thought about kissing him. Not exactly appropriate for a guy she barely knew—but he was cute.

Her eyes drifted to the five-o'clock shadow on his chin. Certain she'd been caught staring, she unfolded her napkin and placed it on her lap.

"Enjoy your meal," Jenny said and scurried off.

Mia should be looking for her phone, but hunger won out. She knifed jelly on a roll and bit into the warm orange-flavored dough. Wickedly scrumptious. She drank from a crystal glass. "The lemonade's sour." A pound of sugar wouldn't take away the tartness.

He held up a crystal bowl. "Want some sugar?"

"Please." She should use Sweet'N Low but being on vacation why not splurge a little? She added three generous teaspoons, deciding she'd make up for her indulgences at spin class on Monday. "What do you do?"

"Do?" His brow rose, and he looked at her like she asked him to explain the theory of relativity.

"Your job."

"Me? I'm a cowhand." His drawl came out a bit over exaggerated.

Her dad regularly watched old westerns. This guy had a casual Gary Cooper presence. She focused on the jagged scar on his chin. She liked the flaw, showed he wasn't plastic-perfect. "Where's your ranch?"

"It's not mine." He winced for a flash. "I'm the foreman of Los Flores Ranch."

The hot cowboy sitting across from her lived in the next town over. Moving back to her hometown suddenly had a big advantage, namely him. She could see him working on the ranch on the outskirts of Hesperia. Lifting bales of hay would explain his beefy arms.

She'd have to give him her number before she left.

TIME TO SAVE A COWBOY

If you enjoyed FIREBRAND'S CUPID, you might want to read COWBOY'S CUPID from my Love's Magic Series.

A Forbidden Love

When Cupid's arrow accidentally strikes the wrong cowboy, she's supposed to fix her mistake—not fall for the alluring mortal.

Cami Calypso receives her first assignment just in time for the Valentine season. As a newbie Cupid Archer, her life is perfect until her arrow accidentally strikes the wrong man. She has sixty days to secure a job as his housekeeper on a ranch and find the cowboy his soul mate—not keep him for herself.

Rhett Holloway needs a housekeeper and cook.

He doesn't need an adorable blonde to distract him.

He doesn't need her to fix his love life.

But here she is, and he finds her irresistible.

EXCERPT

Rhett had a strange feeling in his gut during dinner. Cami kept checking her watch. He'd asked what bothered her, but she said everything was fine.

After a long day, he helped her clean up the dinner dishes, and they walked to her apartment. Her stance was rigid, her body tense. She didn't shift toward him as he strode with his arm around her shoulder.

"What's wrong?"

"I need to tell you something." She shrugged but wouldn't look at him.

They'd only known each other close to two months, but his heart was all in. He unlocked the apartment door. Seated at the edge of the couch, Cami put a distance between them and avoided eye contact.

"Go ahead." He stood by the kitchen table and waited for a response.

"We were never meant to be together," she said, still not looking his way.

His chest tightened. She was breaking up with him.

"I've got a secret. When I show you, I hope you'll still love me."

"Whatever you've done in the past doesn't matter. We'll get through it." He'd made his share of mistakes.

She extracted a glass vial from her pocket. It sparkled and shimmered. "It's not what I've done, it's what I am."

"What are you?" He didn't even see a flicker of a smile.

Her lips tightened into a grimace. "Please listen carefully to what I say."

"All right. Spill." He tapped the side of his pants.

She licked her lips and took a deep breath. "I told you I was a Cupid when you took me to the archery range."

"Okay."

She folded her arms. "I live in Zeus' Kingdom up in the clouds."

His teeth ground, as he sat next to her and said sarcastically, "Of course you do."

"You've seen my archery skills. Even said I was talented." She lifted her chin and blew out a breath. "I am a Cupid, a real live Cupid."

"That's crazy." Maybe she was crazy. His primal instinct told him to leave, but he couldn't move.

"My occupation is an archer." Tears pooled in her eyes. "I'm telling you the truth."

"If you're leaving me, say so, and quit making up this lame story."

"I don't want to go anywhere." She twirled a curl around her finger.

"You don't? And here I thought you were breaking up with me."

"If only things were different. I've got to return home." She looked at her watch.

"So, you are leaving me? Why?" He was confused.

"I don't want to. I'm happy here." Her body slumped, her chin dropped. "My whole life I've dreamed of being good enough."

"But you are good enough." She was the best thing to ever happen to him. "You're perfect for me."

"Don't make me cry. Please let me finish." Her eyes softened. "I've dreamed of visiting Earth and infusing humans with arrows of love. When I got my first earthly assignment, I hit the wrong man, namely you."

Those blue eyes. "You shot me with your arrow of love?"

"It was a mistake. My assignment ducked, and I hit you instead. I was sent to rectify my mishap and set you up with your soulmate. We were never supposed to fall in love."

"You love me." His spirits soared.

"Yes."

"'Bout time you admitted it." He moved closer, but she backed up, out of his reach.

"Will you accept the real me?"

"What do you mean? The real Cami's right in front of me."

"Watch." Rocking back and forth on her heels, her cheeks flushed to a rosier red.

His eyes riveted to her hands.

She unscrewed the glass vial and poured out a glittery substance. Iridescent pink dust swirled and surrounded her. Her body shrunk to the size of a doll, dressed in a shimmering gown. Iridescent wings formed at her shoulders. She flew up midway between the floor and the ceiling.

"Holy shit!" He stared, not frightened, confused.

"I'm a C-Cupid." Her words came out broken.

He froze, became immobile. "This can't be happening."

"I love you, always will." She hovered close to him, and he felt her lips kiss his cheek.

"It's unreal."

"Tell me about it." Her eyes were wide. Wary.

"You really are a Cupid?"

"Yes. Do you still love me?"

He didn't know what to think. "It's too much." He turned his back to her, put his head in his hands.

His girlfriend—a ruler-sized pixie. It couldn't be true.

Except he'd seen her.

Romance Novels by Niki Mitchell

COWBOY'S CUPID
TIME TO SAVE THE COWBOY
REBEL'S CUPID
TIME FOR LOVE
LOVE'S HIGH TIDE
FIREBRAND'S CUPID

Romantic Short Stories Included in Anthologies by Niki Mitchell

LARIATS, LETTERS, AND LACE, "Chantilly's Choice"

Children's Books by Niki Mitchell

KURIOUS KATZ
KURIOUS KATZ AND THE BIG MOVE
KURIOUS KATZ AND THE PLAY DAY
KURIOUS KATZ AND THE NEW FRIEND
KURIOUS KATZ AND THE BIRTHDAY PARTY
KURIOUS KATZ AND THE HALLOWEEN COSTUMES
KURIOUS KATZ AND THE CHRISTMAS TREE
KURIOUS KATZ AND THE BEST CHRISTMAS EVER
FOSTER CATS: ARTEMIS AND HER SNEAKY BROTHER HERCULUES
KURIOUS KATZ AND THE FOURTH OF JULY
KURIOUS KATZ AND THE VALENTINE SURPRISE
KURIOUS KATZ AND THE SNICKERDOODLE STORY

Coming in 2021

Precious Pups: Breezy, the Labrador retriever

Dear Readers,

Thank you for reading TIME FOR LOVE.

I hope you enjoyed my story as much as I enjoyed writing it. Won't you please consider leaving a review? Even just a few works would help others decide if the book is right for them.

Best regards and thank you in advance.

Niki Mitchell

I look forward to hearing from my readers.
Visit me at
https://nikimitchell.weebly.com/
Follow me on FaceBook
author Niki J. Mitchell
Twitter Niki Mitchell@NikiMitchell7
Instagram
NikiJMitchellAuthor

ABOUT THE AUTHOR

Niki Mitchell writes children's books along with contemporary fantasy and historical time-travel romance. She was born in Chicago, Illinois, and moved to Whittier, California in first grade. With a houseful of books and a local library located a few short blocks, her love of reading began at a young age.

Married for over thirty years and a romantic at heart, she enjoys writing about strong female characters in unusual settings. When she isn't playing with her cats, she enjoys reading, taking walks, water aerobics, photography, and traveling.

www.ingramcontent.com/pod-product-compliance
Lightning Source LLC
Chambersburg PA
CBHW030355310726
48979CB00001B/312

* 9 7 8 1 9 5 1 5 8 1 2 3 7 *